MURDER MOTEL

THE KELLYS 1

NIC SAINT

PUSS IN PRINT PUBLICATIONS

MURDER MOTEL

The Kellys 1

Copyright © 2018 by Nic Saint

All rights reserved. No part of this book may be reproduced in any form by any electronic or mechanical means including photocopying, recording, or information storage and retrieval without permission in writing from the author.

This is a work of fiction. Names, characters, places, brands, media, and incidents are either the product of the author's imagination or are used fictitiously. The author acknowledges the trademarked status and trademark owners of various products referenced in this work of fiction, which have been used without permission. The publication/use of these trademarks is not authorized, associated with, or sponsored by the trademark owners.

Edited by Chereese Graves

www.nicsaint.com

Give feedback on the book at: info@nicsaint.com

facebook.com/nicsaintauthor
@nicsaintauthor

First Edition

Printed in the U.S.A

CHAPTER 1

The car was moving along at a snail's pace. The snow was coming down hard now, and the freeway had become practically impossible to navigate. Tom Kelly was still determined to soldier on, though, in spite of the warnings from his family. He'd promised Dee and the kids he'd get them to Cincinnati safe and sound and he'd be damned if he was going to fail them.

"Honey, you have to pull over," his wife was saying, repeating the same mantra she'd stuck to for the past ten miles. "It's not safe to be out in this weather!"

"Yeah, Dad, quit trying to act like you're Liam Neeson in *Taken 4: The Snow Apocalypse*," said his son Scott. At twelve, Scott rarely took his eyes off his iPhone, and the fact that he hadn't even glimpsed at the thing since this deluge began was a testament to how bad the weather had become.

"Isn't there a motel where we can stay until the storm blows over?" Maya asked. She was petting the Kellys' Goldendoodle Ralph, who was howling like a wolf, his nose in the air.

"I think he needs to pee," said Dee. "And as a matter of fact so do I."

"We'll pee when we get there," said Tom, his face practically plastered to the windshield now, hunched over the wheel and praying he wouldn't hit something.

"I'm not going to pee when I get there, Tom. I'm going to pee now," his wife insisted.

It was just a trick to get him to pull over, he knew. They'd stopped less than an hour ago, and he hadn't seen her drink anything so it was physically impossible for her bladder to be full already. The dog was another matter entirely. If he had to go, he had to go, and if he wasn't able to keep it in, he'd let it out on the back seat of the car, which, since it was a rental, he didn't advocate.

"All right, all right, all right," he grumbled.

At forty-eight Tom Kelly, or Professor Kelly to his economics students back at the University of Washington, looked younger than his years, with his floppy brown hair, square chin and engaging smile. He wasn't smiling now, though, more like trying to keep it together, his fingers gripping the wheel until they were white at the knuckles and fervently praying the weather gods would show them some much-needed clemency. "What does the weather forecast say?" he asked for the umpteenth time. "Scott?"

"Sorry, Dad," Scott said. "No reception. Must be the storm."

Which would explain why his son had suddenly lost interest in his precious phone.

"There!" said Dee, pointing to some to-him-invisible spot in the distance.

"There what?" he asked, struggling to remain calm and poised.

"Don't you see the sign? There's a motel up ahead."

"How far?" asked Maya, nervously shuffling in her seat.

"No idea. Must be close, though, right? Otherwise why put up a sign?"

Tom quickly glanced back to the dog, who was still howling at regular intervals. "Maybe we should stop now? Give him a chance to lift his hind leg against a tree?"

"And freeze his tush off? No way, Dad," said Maya, who was Ralph's biggest fan. The feeling was mutual, because Ralph now shoved his wet nose into Maya's neck, causing her to giggle. "Stop it, you big hairy goofball," she said, playfully pushing the dog away.

At seventeen, Maya was the spitting image of her mother: willowy, blond and absolutely stunning, with her mother's striking green, gold-flecked eyes.

"Dad? I got some bad news," said Scott.

"What is it?" Tom asked. He thought he'd reached his quota of bad news for the day.

"Is it the baby?" asked Dee, panic making her voice squeaky. "Is something wrong with the baby?"

"Jacob's fine," said Scott, patting the baby carrier. "Sleeping like a log. Thing is, I gotta pee, too, Dad, and I don't think I can hold it in until Cincinnati, wherever Cincinnati is."

"I told you not to drink so much soda," said his sister. "You're like a camel when you see a can of soda."

"I am not," said Scott indignantly. "I was thirsty."

"Then drink water. You know soda's bad for you."

"I don't like water. Water's got no taste. I hate it."

"Sugar kills your brain cells. And you don't have that many to begin with."

"I've got plenty of brain cells. I can afford to lose a couple hundred."

"Yeah, but can you afford to lose a couple million? I don't think so."

"Kids, not now," said Dee. "Your father is trying to get us out of this mess."

And their father was indeed trying to do just that. Unfortunately the storm and the snow were winning and he and the bright red rental Toyota Highlander was losing.

Just then, a huge sign announcing the presence of the Gateway Lodge Motel loomed up by the side of the road, momentarily visible through a gap in the drifting snow.

Making an executive decision, Tom steered the vehicle onto the off-ramp and in the direction of warmth, comfort and, hopefully, decent sanitary facilities for human and dog.

Others had decided on the same tack, however, with an actual traffic jam as a consequence.

"Why don't we just leave the car, Dad?" Scott suggested. "It's just a rental anyway."

Maya laughed. "That's such a dumb thing to say."

"Who are you calling dumb, bird-face?"

"You can't just leave a rental car by the side of the road, pea-brain."

"Kids," said Dee, trying to inject a parental note of steel into her voice and failing.

"It's a rental!" Scott said. "You simply call the rental company, tell them you had to dump the car because of *force majeure* and that's it. They got LoJack installed on all the cars in their fleet anyway, so all they need to do is look up the car's location, send a flatbed tow truck and that's it." He pointed a finger at his sister. "That's what you pay insurance for."

Maya was shaking her head. "You are such a dumbass."

"No, it's an actual fact. Look it up. I'm right, aren't I? Dad?"

Tom, even though he was proud that Scott was aware of the word 'force majeure,' felt that he needed to set the record straight. "I'm afraid it's not, Scott. Rental companies don't like it when you simply dump their cars by the side of the road. It's gonna cost us."

"This isn't one of your geeky movies, Scott," said Maya, still laughing.

"Well, I need to pee so I'm getting out," said Scott, and opened the door.

An icy gust of wind, along with a few shovels of snow, decided otherwise, and he quickly closed the door again, much to his sister's amusement. He stuck out his tongue.

"Very mature, Scott," she said. "Maybe we should get you one of Jacob's diapers."

Finally, the cars moved on, and quickly Tom managed to reach the motel parking lot. He directed the rental and its long-suffering passengers to the motel entrance, and parked as close as he could. When he finally cut the engine, the Kellys all blew out sighs of relief.

"We're here," Tom announced, quite unnecessarily, since by then the others were already climbing out of the car, leaving him the last one to leave the proverbial sinking ship.

CHAPTER 2

The traffic jam wasn't confined to the freeway, the off-ramp, or even the parking lot. Inside the Gateway Lodge the situation was the same, with lots of people having had the exact same idea as the Kellys. The receptionist, a vivacious young woman with a blond bob and bright red lips, was working as fast as she could, but she had a pretty big crowd to contend with, and Dee had a sinking feeling it might take ages before their turn came.

Meanwhile, at least, the motel bathroom was available, even though there, too, a line had formed. Leaving Tom in charge of both Ralph's leash and the baby carrier, Dee hurried off after her son and daughter, who clearly didn't share her compunction to leave everything to their father.

Then again, when one had to go, one had to go.

She and Maya were next in line, while Scott had already disappeared inside the men's restroom long before.

"What is it about men that makes them so much faster than us?" asked Dee as she darted nervous glances back at Tom, now cradling the baby in one arm while holding onto the dog's leash with the other.

"Simple. It's all down to biology and real estate," said Maya.

She turned to her daughter. Maya's long blond tresses were neatly tucked away inside a white knitted cap, and her face was flushed from the cold.

"Biology and real estate?" Dee asked. "What do you mean?"

"Men pee standing up, which means restroom designers can fit a lot more prime real estate into the same square footage as women's restroom designers, since women need a stall, not a urinal." She shrugged. "The solution most men would suggest is that women simply agree to pee standing up, using a pee funnel." She scoffed. "Typical male thinking. Can you see women dragging a pee funnel around in their purse just in case they need it?"

Dee blinked. It was a topic she had never contemplated in depth.

"My solution? Do away with male and female restrooms, create single, big restrooms with only stalls and no urinals and voila! Problem solved."

"Oh-kay," said Dee carefully. She was still trying to figure out how they were going to reschedule their flight out of Cincinnati and how much this was going to cost, and pee funnels and bathroom architecture were not at the forefront of her mind right now.

Maya tapped her temple. "See? It takes a woman to think these things through and come up with practical solutions to a practical problem."

"That's great, honey," said Dee. She'd taken out her phone and was trying to figure out if she had cell phone reception or Wi-Fi or both. Cell phone reception? Nope. Wi-Fi. Yes!

By the time it was finally Dee's turn, Scott was already walking out of the bathroom, whistling a tune. Maybe her daughter was right, Dee thought briefly. Maybe public bathroom designers needed to take a leaf from Maya's page and do some creative thinking.

But five minutes later she'd finally done her business, washed her hands, splashed some water onto her face, and had forgotten about the whole thing.

She joined her family, and saw that they'd already moved to second in line, the receptionist looking increasingly harried as more and more people poured into the motel.

"So. We need to decide what we're going to do," said Dee. "Stay the night or brave the storm."

"Duh, Mom," said Scott. "That's a no-brainer. This storm is going to wipe us out." He was gesturing at the plate-glass windows to the wintry scene outside. Scott was right. The weather had gotten even worse while they were in there, with snowdrifts up to a foot, and visibility so bad she couldn't even see the rental, even though it was parked right outside.

"If we stay here we're going to have to reschedule our flight," she said.

"No need," said Tom. He turned to the man waiting in line in front of them. He was an elderly florid-faced rotund man with a friendly smile. He was accompanied by an equally rotund woman of similar age and blessed with the same kindly features.

"Hi there," said the man. "Jim Grive. And this is my wife Eden."

"Hi," said Eden, holding out a hand. "Flights out of Cincinnati are all cancelled due to the storm, I'm afraid."

"How do you know?" asked Dee, surprised.

Eden pointed to a television mounted near the ceiling behind the reception desk. Even though it was muted, there was a news ticker running along the bottom of the screen, indicating, 'BLIZZARD WARNING - ALL FLIGHTS OUT OF CINCINNATI AIRPORT CANCELLED.'

"Yeah, that should do it," said Jim, staring up at the screen. "They're saying it might take three days for the storm to blow over and the runways to be cleared."

"What about other airports?" asked Dee.

"Pretty much the same," said Eden. "Dayton's closed, too, and so is Lexington. Same with Louisville, Indianapolis or Columbus. Besides, the roads are a bust, too."

"Yeah, looks like we're stuck out here in lovely..." Jim frowned. "I don't even know where the heck we are."

"Middletown," said his wife, who was starting to display the qualities of a minor oracle. "Just forty miles from our destination. But at least we're inside where it's safe and warm." She smiled at the baby carrier. "You've got a lovely family. How old is the baby?"

"Just eighteen months," said Dee. She looked at her husband. "So we're staying?"

"Seems like the only option. Like Eden just said, at least it's safe and warm."

Dee had expected groans of annoyance and frustration from Maya and Scott, but they were both surprisingly resigned. One look outside told her why this was: even a twelve-year-old couldn't blame the incoming blizzard on his parents, grownups in general, or whoever else he usually shifted the blame for anything bad onto.

Looked like they were extending Thanksgiving Break with one final surprise stop in lovely Middletown. Not that they would see a lot of the small town's no doubt stunning scenery. At least there was a nice, big Christmas tree set up in a corner of the small lobby of the Gateway Lodge Motel. Its many-colored lights twinkled merrily, trying its absolute darndest to spread some of that festive cheer and joy in these bleak circumstances. It warmed Dee's heart and suddenly made her feel like everything might just turn out fine after all.

Just then, a howl made them all look down at Ralph, who was looking up at them with his sad brown eyes. Oh, God, Dee thought. They'd totally forgotten about poor Ralph's bathroom break!

CHAPTER 3

Scott was in hell. No doubt about it. Stuck in the middle of nowhere. Worse. Stuck with his parents and his sister in the middle of nowhere. Worse! Stuck in some crappy motel with his parents and his sister in the arse end of nowhere, like the Brits liked to say.

Aargh!

Why did they have to land themselves in the snowstorm to end all snowstorms? And why was he the one singled out to take Ralph out for a pee in this horrible weather?

Double aargh!

He stomped his feet, the collar of his winter jacket turned up, while he waited for the family Goldendoodle to do his business in the bushes that lined the motel parking lot.

Cars were still pulling in from the highway, the motel their last resort destination, and Scott looked moodily on, while Ralph seemed in no hurry whatsoever to do his business.

"Come on, boy," he said encouragingly. "Just pick a nice bush and take a wee."

But Ralph was a picky dog. He seemed to be determined

to sample every last bush out there before taking his pick. Meanwhile the snow kept on coming down, covering the world in a thick pack of white and frost, and the wind kept on howling, smacking wetly against Scott's exposed face. In spite of his thick parka, his knitted fleece-lined cap and his winter gloves, he was freezing his tush off. Not so Ralph, whose tail was wagging excitedly, poking his nose into a bank of snow and leisurely pawing at the fluffy white stuff.

"Ralph!" Scott said desperately. "Just do it already, boy. Just go ahead and pick a bush. They're all exactly the same and they're all fit for duty."

Ralph turned his head and gave an excited woofle.

"Yeah, yeah, yeah," Scott muttered. He looked up at the sky and allowed the snowflakes to drift down on his face. In spite of the cold he had to admit it was pretty neat. Not that he didn't get enough snow in Seattle, where he lived, but a snowstorm like this was something else. It was as if the world had completely turned white—covering everything.

So he took out his phone, and snapped a couple of selfies against the backdrop of the motel, took another few shots of Ralph as he dug into the snow, and of Ralph as he finally got wise and did his business, digging up some snow to cover the end result.

"Good boy," said Scott, fluffing up the Goldendoodle's ears and getting a happy bark and a lick on the nose in return. "Now let's get inside, shall we? I can't feel my feet."

Returning indoors, he quickly checked the pictures he'd taken. Pretty cool stuff. He posted a couple of them online, then shoved the phone back into his pocket. He had to admit that being out in the cold and watching Ralph enjoy the snow had considerably lifted his mood. And it was with a light heart that he joined his family, hoping that at least they'd picked a nice room for him with a decent flatscreen, some primo cable and other amenities.

Maya couldn't believe her ears. "No separate rooms? You can't be serious!"

"Maya, please," said her mother. "Keep your voice down."

"Mom, I can't be in the same room with that animal," she said, and she didn't mind who heard her. "He makes weird sounds in his sleep! And what's more, he's a hormonal teenager and you know what that means."

"No, I don't know what that means and I don't care," said Mom, who was obviously very near the end of her tether. "We're very lucky they have a room left, so…" She turned to the harried-looking receptionist, who was chewing her bottom lip and nervously glancing at the long row of people still to be processed. "We'll take it. And thank you very much, Vikki."

The young woman brightened. "So that's settled then? Can I have your credit card, Mrs. Kelly?"

Tom, who was still cradling Jacob, gestured silently at his fanny pack, and Maya watched her mother remove Dad's wallet, take out the credit card and hand it to the receptionist.

"This is a disaster," Maya muttered. The prospect of having to share a bed with her brother was horrifying. "How long do we have to stay here for? Please tell me it's just the one night."

"They're saying the storm will last at least three days," said Vikki while she processed Dad's card, then printed out a room key. "Tomorrow will be even worse than today." She pushed her hair away from her face, then produced a weary smile. "Thank you for your business, Mr. and Mrs. Kelly."

"How many rooms have you got left?" asked Maya, not to be deterred.

Vikki grimaced and whispered, "Only three." She glanced at the line of people and Maya got the picture.

She groaned as they stepped away from the counter.

"Looks like we got here just in time," said Mom.

"I wonder what all these people are going to do," said Dad.

"Eden said the Middletown fire department and the Red Cross are setting up a shelter in the high school gym and at people's homes in town."

"What about other hotels?" asked Scott, who'd rejoined them. "There must be plenty of hotels in the area."

"All full," said Mom. "It's a miracle this motel still had a few rooms left."

"Probably because it's a dump," said Scott. "So what room did you get me?"

"We're all in the same room, Scott," said Dad. He handed the baby to Mom. "Now help me get the bags out of the car, will you? Before this blizzard snows it under completely."

Scott stared at his dad. "The same room? You mean me and duck-face have to share a room?"

"Be nice to your sister," said Dad automatically.

"We *all* have to share a room, poo-brain," said Maya with a slight grin. The look on her brother's face almost made it worth it to suffer the intolerable cruelty of being cooped up with the rest of her family in the same room for three days.

"All of us? In one room? No way!" Scott cried.

"At least we're in a room," said Maya. "But if you prefer to spend the next three nights on a camping cot in some high school gym be my guest. At least I won't have to live through the horror of sharing a bed with my idiot brother."

"Sharing a bed! You gotta be joking!" Scott looked absolutely horrified now, and it was gratifying to know that Maya wasn't the only one going through hell right now.

"Scott," Dad said. "Come on, dude. Let's get that luggage before it's too late."

And as Scott and Dad walked away, Maya could hear her brother loudly complain about this latest tragedy that had befallen him.

"Teenagers," she said. "Can't live with them. Can't kill them."

Mom grinned, then immediately wiped away her smile. Parenting 101: never give the impression of partiality, especially by appearing to approve when one kid lambasts another.

"Come on," Mom said. "Let's find our room, before someone else gets there first."

Maya, holding the leash Scott had relinquished, tugged it and Ralph gave a cheerful bark.

At least one member of this family was happy with this unexpected adventure.

CHAPTER 4

Tom looked around the room and was pretty shocked to discover it was about as big as his home office, or possibly even a touch smaller. There were two double beds crammed in there, or at least that's what he thought they were, as to him they appeared smaller than a double bed ought to be, a table smushed against the window with two chairs, and an old TV set dumped on a cabinet at the foot of one of the beds. The wallpaper, peeling in places, was an ugly green, the nightstands were plywood and they, too, were shedding parts of their anatomy, and the whole thing gave him a distinct sense of overwhelming sadness.

Still he managed to smile in the face of adversity. Courage under fire. "And here we are," he caroled loudly, anticipating the torrent of hell that was about to rain down on his and Dee's heads. "Our new home away from home. Nice and cozy. Snug like a bug in a rug." And to add some jollity to the occasion, and attempt to defuse the situation before it detonated, he jumped onto the bed closest to the door. "I got dibs on this one, you guys!"

When the expected torrent of rage and disappointment

didn't come, he looked back and saw that the rest of the family was still standing there, mouths agape, expressions of utter shock on their faces.

Dee was the first one to recover. She plastered a fake smile on her face and said, "Ooh. This looks so cozy. I think I'm gonna love it here."

"This is so wrong," said Maya, taking in the room.

"This is hell," her brother chimed in. "I just landed in hell."

"It's not so bad," said Tom. "It's better than being out there in the storm of the century." Before his offspring could launch into a tirade he picked up the remote and flicked on the TV. It flickered to life with obvious reluctance and displayed footage from WKRC, which appeared to be the local CBS affiliate. A woman reporter dressed like an Eskimo was standing in front of what looked like a big church, shouting into the wind, snow swirling all around her, making it hard to see where she was, exactly.

"At least they got Wi-Fi," Scott muttered, and flung himself onto the other bed, took out his phone, and was soon lost to the world.

Maya threw up her arms. "Really? I have to sleep in *that* with *that*? What about privacy, Dad? No way am I going to share a bed with that *animal*!"

Tom shared a look with his wife. "I'll sleep here with Maya, how about that?" Dee suggested. "That way the boys can bunk together and so can the girls. Deal?"

Maya nodded morosely. "Thanks, Mom. At least someone around here knows how to keep their heads together in a crisis."

Ralph, meanwhile, was sniffing at Tom's feet, also looking for his place in this entirely new constellation, and Jacob, opening his eyes for the first time since they'd arrived at the motel, looked around at his new environment, fixed his eyes on Maya, who was bending over the baby carrier, puckered up his face and started wailing.

"I'll take him," said Maya when Dee made to pick the baby up from the carrier.

"He probably needs a new diaper," muttered Dee.

Maya gave her mother a weak smile. "Why don't I take care of that for you?"

"Thanks, honey," said Dee gratefully.

They watched as Maya disappeared into the bathroom, a fresh diaper in hand, then came walking out again five seconds later. "This place is filthy, Dad. Absolutely gross."

Tom got up from the bed and walked into the bathroom. His daughter was right. There was hair in the shower, toothpaste smeared to the sink, and when he opened the flimsy plastic toilet lid a perfectly shaped turd was staring back at him. "Oh, Christ," he muttered as he let the toilet lid drop back into place.

For the first time since they'd arrived he felt anger bubbling up inside of him.

This was too much. It took a lot to make mild-mannered Professor Kelly upset but now they'd done it. There was nothing he hated more than a total lack of hygiene.

He stalked out of the bathroom and back into the tiny room, picked up the phone from the nightstand and dialed the lobby. "May I please speak with the manager?" he informed politely when the same harried receptionist snatched up the phone. "Now, please?" he added when she said the manager was unfortunately very busy right now.

The eyes of his family on him, Tom raised himself up to his full height when the manager's voice finally sounded on the other end.

"Yes, this is Thomas Kelly. Professor Thomas Kelly. I'm afraid that the room we've been assigned is an absolute disgrace, sir." His voice was shaking when he spoke the next words. "There is a turd in the toilet, sir. A turd!"

Another ten minutes later there was a knock at the door and the manager strode in. He was a short man with only a few token strands of hair still attached to his round dome. He had large, slightly protruding eyes and heavy brows, which gave him a distinctly weird look. When he spoke, though, it was with the quiet efficiency and cool authority customary to one in his position.

"Please show me the turd," he said, and he wasn't smiling.

Scott, meanwhile, was softly chuckling from his position on the bed, Maya had a hard time suppressing a grin, too, and even Jacob had halted his wailing long enough to produce a soft gurgle that could or could not be interpreted as an expression of mirth.

In absolute silence, his dour demeanor befitting the gravity of the situation, Tom led the way into the bathroom, pointed ostentatiously at the hair in the shower drain, the toothpaste smears in the sink and, finally, with a flourish, he threw the toilet lid back and stood to the side while the manager inspected the offending turd.

The man's brows puckered together into a frown, and, if possible, his eyes protruded even further. For a moment Tom thought they'd depart from their parent body but they appeared to have been affixed sufficiently to prevent such a calamity from happening.

"Myes," the manager finally spoke. "You are absolutely right, Professor. This is an outrage. Unfortunately I'm not in a position to assign you another room, as the motel is booked solid, but I will send the cleaner in here to take care of this." He was fixedly staring at the turd as if attempting to identify the person who'd produced the offending object, but finally gave up and dropped the lid back down.

He stood, rigid and formal. "Accept my deepest apologies,

Professor. I will, of course, comp you your room. The Gateway Lodge Motel has certain standards and this, I can assure you, is not up to our usual standards. At least not as long as I'm in charge."

Tom, mollified by the way the motel manager was handling this minor emergency, softened. "That's all right. These things happen. And under the circumstances I can understand how your cleaner could have overlooked the previous guest's... donation."

"That is most kind of you, Professor Kelly," said the manager, giving a slight nod. "But still unacceptable. I'm sure there must have been some kind of oversight and I will deal with this matter straight away. You have my word this will never happen again."

"Thank you," said Tom, gratified that his complaint had been given the attention it deserved. Suddenly feeling predisposed to chat, he relaxed. "So you're booked solid, huh?"

"Absolutely full," said the manager, stepping out of the bathroom, followed by Tom, and nodding a kindly greeting to the rest of the family, who were still having a hard time suppressing their hilarity. "It's been a hellish day but we're coping as best we can."

"How much longer will the storm last?" asked Dee from the bed.

"Three days at the most," said the manager.

"Do you have enough food to last us three days?" asked Scott, voicing a concern that must have just sprung to mind.

The manager smiled indulgently. "Of course. We have plenty of provisions, young man. In fact we have enough food to feed a small army so we should be absolutely fine. Where are you fine folks from?"

"Seattle," said Tom.

The little man rocked back on his perfectly polished black brogues. "The emerald city, eh? I've never been but everyone tells me Seattle is a wonderful place to visit. The Space Needle. The monorail. Pike Place Market. One of these days I'll have to make the trip."

"Actually we live in a small town right next to Seattle," said Dee. "It's called Medina."

The manager smiled. "It's an honor to have you in my humble abode, Kellys," he said. "And now if you will excuse me… A manager's work is never finished." He nodded a greeting to Tom. "Professor Kelly. Mrs. Kelly. Kids." He directed a slightly censorious look at Ralph, then left the room.

The moment he'd stepped out, both Scott and Maya roared with laughter. Tom smiled as he shared a look of relief with his wife. So far so good, that look said.

CHAPTER 5

*V*ernon Haggis, manager of the Gateway Lodge, stalked away from Room 21D with a deep groove cut between his brows, his mood mimicking the dropping temperatures outside. Motels like the Gateway had a reputation for being less than clean but when he'd assumed managerial duties of the place fifteen years before he'd vowed not to allow the Gateway to fall into the same trap. He didn't see why a motel should be a fleabag. In fact he saw no reason why a motel couldn't offer the same fine experience a five-star hotel did.

Everything began with the staff you engaged, of course, and that's where Vernon's problems lay. The staff of the Gateway was not the kind of staff the Hilton or the Ritz-Carlton attracted. People yearned to work at the Hilton or the Ritz-Carlton. They dreamed of being connected with the brand—with the class and the fine reputation for excellence.

They didn't have such lofty dreams when they applied for a job at the Gateway Lodge.

Muttering to himself, he soon arrived back in the lobby, where poor Vikki Mammal was still slaving away, trying to get those final few people assigned rooms. The rest of them would sadly have to be denied lodgings. Vernon had been in contact with the other hotels in town, all of them fully booked, with the only alternative set up by the fire department at Middletown High.

Or people could brave the storm and head to the next town, which was unwise.

Vernon quickly counted heads, then cleared his throat to attract the attention of the small gathering. When all eyes had turned to him, he said, "I'm afraid the Gateway Lodge is now fully booked." Over the murmur of disapproval, he added, "The only other option at the moment is Middletown High, where the fire department and the Red Cross are organizing a shelter. There are also some of our local families who have volunteered to open up their homes and offer temporary lodging until this terrible storm has blown over. Those of you who would like to stay in town, please raise your hands."

There were plenty of people ready to take Middletown up on its offer, he saw, and he nodded to Leroy Burg, Mayor Burg's son and a volunteer with the Red Cross. Leroy held up his spindly arms and raised his reedy voice. "Hey, you guys! We've organized a bus to take you to the shelter. A snowplow will accompany us and clear the road as best it can. But we have to leave now, before the storm gets worse. So please grab your bags and your loved ones and organize yourselves. The bus will be leaving in ten minutes. Ten minutes, people."

Satisfied the minor evacuation was well underway, Vernon proceeded in the direction of the kitchen, where his chef and staff were now going to have to contend with plenty more people than they were accustomed to. And as he stalked off, his mind abuzz with a million things he still needed to take care of, he thought he saw a man he recognized approaching the front desk. He looked like that famous billionaire Wilbur Hall, owner and proprietor of the Hall-mart chain of supermarkets and discount department stores.

Vernon shook it off. No way one of the richest men in the country would stoop so low as to patronize the Gateway Lodge in Middletown, Ohio. Men like Hall stayed at the poshest hotels in the world. Men like Hall probably *owned* the poshest hotels in the world.

❧

Vikki tucked a strand of hair back into her bob. Her pits were drenched with sweat, her blouse sticking to her back and her legs were hurting from being on her feet for so long. She'd been standing at the front desk for over five hours and she was pretty much beat.

When her shift had started that morning the storm was already raging but she had no idea it would get this bad this quick. Hour after hour she'd been watching the WKRC newscaster get gloomier and gloomier and the forecast get worse and worse. Now, a little past noon, it was so dark out it might just as well have been past six o'clock, and the snow was still falling from the leaden sky, the wind roaring and howling, and WKRC's weatherman spelling doom with each new weather forecast.

She thought about her bike parked in the motel parking space, and how there was no way she was going to be able to get home when her shift was over. Her mom had already called, telling her she'd pick her up, but by now the weather was so bad there was no way she was going to let her mom risk life and limb by driving out here in her crappy old car. She'd only get herself stuck and would have to be rescued by the National Guard or something.

Vernon had already told her she could sleep at the motel for the next couple of days. Same story with the cooks and the rest of the staff. He had a couple of extra rooms on the third floor that needed to be remodeled and weren't fit for paying guests to stay in. Besides, it wasn't as if anyone else was going to come in for work tomorrow. And the guests had to be fed, the rooms cleaned, and the front desk manned in case people needed something. Like a map of the area and some pointers on the funnest things to see in Middletown. Yeah, right. The only thing to see right now was snow, snow, and even more snow!

At least Vernon had assured them there was plenty of food and supplies to last them the three days the storm was supposed to pummel the area, and the Gateway Lodge was a pretty sturdy structure and wouldn't blow away, no matter how hard the storm huffed and puffed.

She glanced down at her phone. Billy had sent another message. He was still mighty upset she'd called off their date tonight. Said if he couldn't rely on her he was going to have 'do some serious thinking about their future together.'

She set her lips and plunked down her phone. What an idiot. Didn't he have eyes in his head? Couldn't he see there was a frickin' blizzard rolling into the area?

A heavyset man approached the desk. He had a gray buzzcut, a perfectly trimmed little mustache and beetling brows. He looked vaguely familiar. And it wasn't because she'd handled his registration. She'd know if she had. She was great with faces. "If you want to register I'm afraid we're full now, sir," she said in her kindliest voice. "But if you talk to that man over there, he's organizing the local shelter and he's leaving in just a few minutes."

But the man waved an annoyed hand. "I'm a guest at the motel, Miss…" He frowned at her name tag.

"Mammal. Vikki Mammal," she said.

"Right," he said dismissively. "The thing is… I'm here with my daughter and we were supposed to meet her fiancé. We were going to drive into the city and take a flight out to Arkansas. Only so far he hasn't shown up. And now I'm worried that with the storm…"

"What's his name? I'll see if he checked in."

"Towns. Donny Towns."

She quickly checked the register on her computer. "I don't have a Mr. Donny Towns staying at the Gateway Lodge I'm afraid, Mr.…"

"Hall. Wilbur Hall."

Her eyes widened slightly. Of course. Wilbur Hall. Owner of the biggest chain of supermarkets in the country. His likeness had been on the cover of *Time Magazine*. He'd even written a book about how to go from zilch to zillionaire in a lifetime. She tried her best to hide her excitement. It didn't do to fawn all over the motel's guests. Then again, it wasn't every day that a man of Hall's stature stayed at the Gateway Lodge. Actually more like never.

Hall hesitated for a moment, fingers drumming on the desk. Then he seemed to make up his mind about something and took out his phone. "What if I showed you his picture? Maybe he's one of the people you had to send away because the motel was full." He swiped at his phone for a moment then held it out in front of Vikki's nose. "Recognize him?"

She did. The picture Wilbur Hall was showing her was none other than Hot Gangster. His mugshot had become an overnight sensation when the NYPD had published it on their Facebook page. Quickly dubbed Hot Gangster on account of the fact that he looked more like a male model than a gangster, women had wanted to date him, men had wanted to be him, and soon after his release he'd gotten a contract with a modeling agency and had become one of the most sought-after catwalk models ever. His face, tattoos and all, now frequently appeared in clothes ads and perfume ads and ads for pretty much everything under the sun.

And then Vikki remembered something else. Wasn't Hot Gangster engaged to be married to the daughter of a very wealthy individual? Of course! He was going to marry Wilbur Hall's daughter, the equally rich and very delectable Tracy Hall, well-known socialite.

She realized Mr. Hall was waiting for her reply, so she quickly nodded. "He's here, Mr. Hall. I checked him in myself. But he didn't use the name Donny Towns." She frowned, trying to recollect what name he had used. At the time she'd thought he looked familiar. "This must have been yesterday, um… before lunch. And I put him in room… 24B." Her fingers were already dancing across the keyboard. "I remember because 24B is the room where we like to put our local celebrities. Politicians, sports stars, people like that. And he looked so familiar I figured he was famous for something, so I decided to put him in 24B." She realized she was babbling when she finally brought up the registration. "There we go," she said, chipper and bright. "He's registered as Mr. Adam Plauder."

And then she saw the anomaly and her eyes widened.

"What?" asked Wilbur Hall, now visibly irate. "What is it?"

She looked up at the man and met his eyes. She saw they were small eyes, buried between the flabby contours of his face, and they were flashing angrily. This was not a man who liked to be kept waiting by lowly receptionists.

"What?!" he demanded.

"He's not alone in that room, Mr. Hall. It's registered to a Mr. *and* Mrs. Plauder."

CHAPTER 6

Dee finally found the plastic container with the baby food she'd prepared at their hotel in Dayton and took it out. Maya had changed Jacob's diaper but he was still crying, which probably meant he was hungry. She gently cradled and rocked the baby in her left arm. His face was red from crying and his dark hair plastered across his little brow. She felt his temperature. Normal. At least he hadn't suffered from the trip up from Dalton or the surprise detour to Middletown and its sterling Gateway Lodge.

Maya had gone downstairs to check out the motel, Scott had taken it upon himself to walk Ralph again, and Tom was reading something on his laptop, his reading glasses perched on the tip of his nose and his face scrunched up into his usual expression of concentration. She knew better than to interrupt him when he was like that. Their vacation over, he was going back to work in a few days, Maya and Scott were going back to school and Dee was returning to the art gallery she ran in Seattle's Pike/Pine neighborhood.

Dee peeled back the lid on the container, dug the spoon in and started feeding Jacob the mashed veggie and potato combo. She hoped the motel would give her access to the kitchen so she could maybe prepare her little darling some choice food later on. This was her last container and then her stash was finished.

Jacob had stopped crying and was munching his food with marked interest. She smiled. "You were hungry, weren't you? That's right," she said as he grabbed at her hand, eager for more of the yummy food. "We're not exactly on the plane home yet but we're getting there."

She glanced out of the window, where the world was wiped away in a complete whiteout by now. She frowned. "Tell me Scott isn't taking Ralph out in this weather."

"They're fine," said Tom. "I told him to stay close to the motel."

"Tom! They'll be blown away!"

"It's not as bad as it looks," Tom muttered.

She got up from her perch on the edge of the bed and walked over to the window. She could hardly see the parking lot. "It looks pretty bad out there, Tom."

"Mh…" was Tom's only response.

"Oh, for God's sakes. Tom!"

He finally looked up, and removed his glasses. "What?"

"You have to go after him. He can't be out there in this weather. He'll freeze!"

Tom smiled, that typical professor's smile that she alternately loved and hated about him. "He won't freeze to death. He just won't!" he cried when she produced a groan of despair. "I told him to dress up properly and to stay close to the motel. He'll be fine."

She was shaking her head, then handed him Jacob and started rummaging around for her coat.

"Oh, Dee, for heaven's sake," said Tom, holding the baby as if he were a live grenade. "You're not going after him, are you?"

"If you're not going after him, I will," she said as she pulled on her thick coat.

"He's a teenager! Everyone knows teenagers are virtually indestructible!"

She didn't even deign that last comment with a reply. Instead she stomped out of the room, hoping she wouldn't find her twelve-year-old buried under a thick pile of snow.

※

Scott inwardly cursed. The Wi-Fi signal was supposed to cover a hundred feet. Well, he wasn't even thirty feet from the entrance to the hotel and already he'd lost the signal. He tucked the phone into his pocket and stared down at Ralph, who, for the second time since they arrived, was digging his nose into a pile of snow and appeared reluctant to do his business.

"Come on," he said. "I know you don't feel the cold but I'm freezing."

The dog had been whining and scratching at the door of their motel room, a clear sign he needed to go, and since Maya was too busy changing the baby's diaper, Dad had something important to do on his laptop and Mom was in charge of Jacob's feeding schedule, it was up to Scott to walk the dog. Again.

When he'd told the others he had better things to do, they'd just shaken their heads and laughed. Well, he had, hadn't he? He was just about to beat Ricki in *Grand Theft Auto: San Andreas* again and now he had to forfeit his hard-won victory so he could take the dog out for a walk.

Ugh. No fair.

The storm had picked up, and the wind was slicing into him, the snow feeling as if it was trying to freeze him alive. But Ralph didn't seem to care. He kept walking out further and further, going from snowdrift to snowdrift, happily sticking his nose into the wet muck.

The cars had finally stopped coming, and the parking lot was deserted now, everyone who needed to be inside safely tucked into the motel, and the others probably in that Red Cross shelter or wherever.

They were at the back of the motel now, where Scott's only view was a few sad trees, their branches heavily laden with snow, part of a small patch of forest. There was something else out there. It was hard to know for sure, what with the blizzard going from strength to strength, but from time to time, when there was a slight lull in the proceedings, he thought he could see a small frozen lake. Would be great for ice skating, he reckoned.

Ralph tugged at the leash and he followed the dog with another tired groan.

"Do your business already, Ralphie," he implored the dog. "Who cares where you do it?"

But the dog wasn't listening. Instead he was digging into yet another snowdrift with a fervor and an energy that was probably better spent on worthier undertakings.

They were right behind the motel now, and when Scott looked up he could see he was standing right beneath one of the rooms, the window obviously closed now.

Ralph was still digging furiously, snow flying in every direction. If he was going to do his business here he was definitely making sure he'd dug a nice deep hole first.

Scott glanced around, bored already. He wondered what he'd do next. Maybe he could entice Ricki for a rematch. That seemed only fair. Extenuating circumstances and all that. Only Ricki had never won before, so he might not want to be up for that. He'd just tell Scott he was a lousy loser and to buzz off. Three more days of this crap. Then a flight and then life would go back to normal, and this vacation of hell was finally over.

Visiting Grandma and Grandpa in Dayton for Thanksgiving had sounded like a lot of fun, until they'd arrived and discovered they had to contend with Uncle Gareth and Aunt Suzie and their five annoying brats—none of whom seemed to like Scott very much. All boys, they'd given him a pretty hard time, and he was glad to be rid of the lot of them.

Ralph was tugging at something. He'd dug his teeth in and was pulling mightily.

"What have you got there, buddy?" asked Scott, curious in spite of himself.

But Ralph wasn't letting go. He pulled and pulled and suddenly there was a rip and the dog flew back, something between his teeth.

Scott sank down on his haunches and held out his hand. "Come here, boy. What have you got?"

Ralph, tail wagging happily, pranced up and dropped a piece of cloth at Scott's feet.

Scott stared at the cloth, then stared into the hole the dog had dug.

And that's when he saw that a man was staring back at him.

CHAPTER 7

Scott jerked up and involuntarily yelped in shock and fear. He landed on his butt in the snow, still staring at the man, who kept staring back, eyes open and frozen and... dead!

Scott yelped again, this time louder. And that's when a woman's cries reached his ear.

"Scott! Where are you? Answer me, Scott!"

Mom came around the corner, trudging through the snow.

He held up his hand. "Over here, Mom," he said.

"Oh, Scottie!" she cried, and hurried in his direction. "Are you all right?"

"I'm fine, Mom. It's just that..." He pointed at the dead man. "He's not fine."

Mom had finally reached him and was helping him to his feet. "What are you talking about? Who?"

But then she saw it, and she, too, produced a loud cry of shock. "What's that?!"

"I think that's a dead man, Mom. And from the looks of things he's been out here for a while."

They both stared down at the man. He wasn't wearing a thick coat or a hat or anything. From what they could see of him he was only dressed in a plaid shirt. Not exactly the dress code for a blizzard, Scott reckoned. "Do you think he was taking his dog for a walk and froze to death?" he asked. "Or maybe he came out here for a smoke?"

Mom seemed to swallow away a lump of uneasiness, then approached the man.

Ralph, meanwhile, sat on his butt, panting happily, like a dog who hasn't just found a bone, but an entire bag of bones. He produced a cheerful woof and Scott patted his head. "Good boy," he muttered. "Good boy."

"He's got something stuck in his chest," said Mom now, hunched over as she studied the dead man. She then looked back at him, an expression of something between awe and shock on her face.

"Stuck to his chest? You mean like a piece of chicken or cheese dip?"

She was shaking her head slowly. "More like… a knife."

Once again reality seemed to elude him, as if it were suddenly operating just slightly outside of his grasp. Like one of those artsy movies Dad liked, where nothing seemed to make sense. "A knife to cut the chicken?"

Mom swallowed once again. "I think he was killed, Scott. Someone stuck a knife in this guy and killed him then left him out here to die."

*

Vernon was stomping his feet in an attempt to keep warm. Pretty soon now night would fall and the blizzard would reach fever pitch. No one was supposed to be outside when that happened. He'd seen *The Day After Tomorrow* and people could simply freeze to death by being exposed to these elements. And now this. A dead body. And not just a dead body but a dead guest. First that turd in Professor Kelly's toilet and now a dead guest.

What a day.

He recognized him, too. It was that famous Hot Gangster. He didn't look so hot now, though. More like Frozen Gangster. Or Iced Gangster, as it was obvious he'd been murdered.

That's what you got from hosting gangsters in your establishment, of course. Sooner or later they bumped into other gangsters and one of them bumped off the other one.

The big question was: why did they have to do it at the Gateway Lodge for crying out loud? Why not take their business to some other hotel in town, or even the mall? Why here?

He stomped his feet some more and blew into his hands. Ravi Fischer, who was the motel's handyman, and Beau Snoop, member of the Gateway waitstaff, were digging the dude out with shovels and had finally managed to remove enough of the snow so they could pull him out of his frosted grave and shift him on top of the wheelbarrow.

Vernon leaned in and grabbed the dead guy's feet. To his surprise he was barefoot. Huh. Weird. He grabbed them and pulled him up while Beau and Ravi did the same with the guy's torso, Ravi hoisting him up by the left arm while Beau took care of the right one.

"Dude's heavy," said Ravi with a grunt.

"Are those... pajamas?" asked Beau.

"Yep. He decided to come out here in his pajamas, get stabbed and die," said Vernon, exasperated. "Just pull, Beau, and stop asking your stupid questions."

"If you ask me, he probably got chucked out of that window up there," said Ravi, gesturing to the window just overhead.

Vernon looked up. "Huh. That's 24B. Was he in 24B? I'll have to ask Vikki."

"He was in 24B all right," said Ravi as they finally reached the wheelbarrow and carefully balanced Mr. Hot Gangster's frozen corpse on top of it. The model-slash-gangster was slightly stooped over, which made for a perfect fit, his butt landing in the barrow's tray.

"How do you know?" asked Beau, catching his breath.

"Because he asked me to look at the boiler. Said the water wasn't hot enough."

Vernon nodded, recollection stirring. "Right, right. And did you? Fix it?"

"Nothing wrong with that boiler. He was in there with some woman and she used up all the hot water. So I told him to wait and then try again. Where do you wanna put him?"

"Kitchen freezer."

"Kitchen freezer!" Beau cried, aghast. "You can't put a dead body in with the food!"

"I can't put a dead body in with the guests," Vernon growled. "And as long as he's frozen he's not gonna contaminate anything now is he?"

"I like your thinking, boss," said Ravi, who was a rough-hewn man with coal shovels for hands and a face like a halibut. "Just don't tell the guests is my advice. They might not like it."

"Of course they won't like it!" Beau cried. Like his name implied, he was a handsome young fellow with butter-colored hair. "Can't we call the cops? They can put him in their freezer."

"Cops won't come," said Vernon. "This blizzard is about to hit and they can't risk coming out here. I just talked to Chief Boelk. He's the one who told me to put him in the freezer for the time being." He sighed and stared out at the mother and son and dog watching the scene from a safe distance. "I just hope the Kellys will keep their trap shut."

"They the ones found Hot Gangster?" asked Ravi.

"Actually their dog found him."

Ravi smiled. "Clever pooch. If not for him we might not have found Mr. Gangster for another couple of weeks, as I normally wait to clear this part of the motel until springtime."

"Yeah, clever pooch," said Vernon, eyeing the pooch in question nastily.

CHAPTER 8

Tom was just wondering where his wife and son had gone off to when Maya came hurrying into the room. "Dad! Ralph found a dead body!"

He shot up in such a hurry he almost dropped the baby. "What?!"

"You better go out there and see for yourself. I'll take care of Jacob."

She took the baby from him and he hurried out before remembering he had no idea where he was going so he hurried back into the room. "Where are they?"

"Out back," said Maya, taking a seat on the bed and switching on the TV. *Die Hard 2* was on, with Bruce Willis having his own snowstorm to contend with.

Tom hurried out again before remembering he was in his slippers and boxers so he hurried back inside, quickly dressing while Maya gave him a critical look, then finally was on his way.

Arriving downstairs, he saw that the same receptionist was still manning the desk. The girl looked pretty much dead on her feet by now. He waved at her and she waved back, plastering a smile onto her face. But when she saw he was heading outside, the smile quickly evaporated. "You can't go out there, Mr. Kelly!" she yelled.

He popped his head back in. "My daughter told me my dog found... something."

She brought a hand to her face, a look of distress sliding over her features. "Oh."

"Out back, right?"

She nodded quickly. "Right underneath 24B," she said for good measure.

There was an odd expression on her face and he filed it away for later use.

The moment he walked out the front door the storm hit him in the face like an icy smack, and for a moment he staggered, almost blown back inside. Christ this blizzard was getting worse by the minute. Darkness had by now descended on the world and he stayed close to the motel as he moved along in the direction indicated.

And that's when he saw the procession: first he saw the hotel manager loom up out of the darkness, snow swirling around his form as he approached. He was pushing something. And when Tom saw what it was he was pushing his stomach suddenly lurched and the granola bar and banana he'd just snacked on decided to play a return date.

He quickly moved out of the way of the trio of men balancing the dead man and the wheelbarrow and then he was upchucking his lunch into the side of a snowed-in car.

"Are you all right, honey?" Dee asked, sidling up to him.

"I'm... fine... now," he said, wiping his lips. She took his arm and steered him back in the direction of the motel.

"Hey, Dad," said Scott, who was holding an excitedly yapping Ralph on the leash. "Ralph found a dead guy. Buried under a pile of snow. Pretty weird, huh?"

He nodded. "Pretty weird," he agreed, his voice a wobble.

He watched the three men move out of sight. They weren't heading for the entrance, though. "Where are they going?" he asked.

"Kitchen entrance," said Scott. "They want to avoid being seen by the guests. I guess dead bodies are bad for business."

"Absolutely," he agreed, and allowed his wife and son to support him as they returned indoors.

Right behind them, as Tom staggered into the lobby, the receptionist quickly locked the door, making sure that from now on no one left the motel.

"Did you see him?" she asked, her eyes wide now.

"Ralph found him," Scott repeated, clearly prepared to tell his tale to anyone who would listen.

"Is he… dead?" the girl asked.

"Dead as a doornail," said Scott with inappropriate glee.

The girl held her hands to her face. "He's a guest."

"Yeah. Hot Gangster," said Scott. "I overheard the manager and the others," he explained to Tom.

"Hot Gangster? Who's Hot Gangster?" asked Tom.

"Don't you remember, Tom?" asked his wife. "He's the gangster whose mug shot was everywhere for a while. On TMZ and *Page Six* and *Star Magazine*. And then when he got involved with Tracy Hall he became even more famous. Those shots of the two of them aboard her daddy's yacht were on the front page of every magazine in the country."

Tom was frowning. "I don't remember reading about him."

"Yeah, I don't think they write about guys like him in the *Wall Street Journal*, Dad," said Scott with a chuckle. "Or even *Forbes Magazine*."

"They write about Wilbur Hall," said the receptionist whose name, according to her name tag, was Vikki Mammal. "Tracy Hall is his daughter. And the weirdest thing? Mr. Hall was looking for his future son-in-law just before. Said they'd arranged to meet and he never showed. And then when I looked I saw he'd registered under a false name along with a woman claiming to be his wife!"

"Oh, cool!" Scott cried, laughing.

"What was the name he registered under?" asked Dee.

"Adam Plauder."

"And the wife?"

Vikki's eyes had gone as wide as saucers. "Oh, God! It's her! It's his real wife! He was cheating on his future wife with his ex-wife!"

CHAPTER 9

"What do you mean, his ex-wife?" asked Scott, who wasn't as up to date on all these celebrity rumors as his mom obviously was.

"I thought I'd seen her before somewhere," said Vikki. "And him, of course. But I didn't make the connection until now. That woman who signed up with him was his ex-wife. The one he divorced when he met Tracy Hall!"

"So the dude was here with his ex-wife and meeting his new wife? Cool!" said Scott.

"Not cool," his father admonished him. "He was cheating on his new wife with his old wife. That's not a cool thing to do, even for a hot gangster."

"Actually Tracy is not his wife," said Mom, who seemed to be on top of this stuff. "They were engaged to be married."

"Well, I guess the wedding is off," said Scott, earning himself another stern look from his father. "I'll take Ralphie upstairs, shall I?" he suggested. "Dog's been through enough."

And as he walked away, he instead swerved in the direction of the kitchen. He'd totally forgotten to take a few shots of Hot Gangster as he was laid up in his wintry grave, what with being all discombobulated and all, but he wasn't going to let this opportunity pass him by to take a couple of quick pics of the dude laid up between tubs of Ben & Jerry's and bags of frozen peas.

He had a pretty good hunch where the kitchen was—just had to follow the signs that pointed to the dining room and keep on going until he saw those typical flapping doors. Ralphie seemed excited about this new adventure, too, for he was panting like the happy poochie-poo he was.

"Good boy," said Scott, patting the dog on the head. "I didn't know you were a cadaver dog, though. Pretty soon now you're going to be finding corpses all over the place."

They'd arrived in the dining room, which was nicely deserted at this time, and Scott quickly drew a bead on the swinging doors with those porthole windows he was looking for. He quickly tiptoed up to them, dragging a proudly prancing Ralph along, and took a quick peek through the round window to see who was on the other side.

To his great joy he saw the hotel manager and his able-bodied assistants as they stood conversing in front of what looked like a giant freezer.

"Bingo," he murmured, and Ralph gave a soft woofle. Dammit!

He ducked down his head, but too late. The door swung open and the hotel manager stood before him, hands planted on his sides and staring at him with all the hostility of one who'd just spotted a fly in the soup. "Young Mr. Kelly," said the manager. "Are you lost?"

"Not really. I just figured I'd, you know, see if there was something I could do."

The manager arched his brows curiously. "Don't tell me your dog has found another dead guest."

"Nah. I figure it's just the one. Though now that you mention it, you might want to look into the dead dude's ex-wife. Apparently they were both staying in 24B, so if he's dead, something might have happened to her, too."

"Unless she killed him," said the second man, who'd joined them. He was big and beefy, with the biggest hands Scott had ever seen on a guy. Probably a baseball pitcher.

"That's for the police to decide," said the manager.

"Yeah, but it'll be three days before they get here. By that time the bird might have flown."

"You want me and Ralph to help you out with the investigation?" Scott suggested. It had just occurred to him that a nice murder investigation might help pass the time.

"No, thank you, young man," said the manager, the corners of his lips curling down in disapproval. "I think you've done enough for one day. You and that dog of yours."

It just might have been Scott's imagination, but it sounded to him as if the manager wasn't happy about Ralph finding that body. And as he walked away, he wondered if the manager might somehow be involved in the murder.

"Young Kelly?" the manager's voice came.

He turned. "It's Scott," he told him.

The manager walked up to him. "Your father. He's a professor, right?"

"Yup. Smartest guy I know."

"He's a professor in Seattle?"

"University of Washington."

The manager seemed to ponder this. "What field is he in?"

Scott was going to say economics when a thought occurred to him. It was one of those bright thoughts that hit you out of nowhere—like a flash! "Criminology," he said. "Dad is the greatest expert on the criminal mind in the world. Cops ask for his advice all the time, and so does the FBI and Homeland Security. Have you seen that show *Mindhunter*?"

"About the FBI—the development of serial-killer profiling?"

"Bingo. They picked my dad's brain when they developed that show. He's only the original profiler."

"Is he indeed?" said the manager, his eyes twinkling as he thoughtfully rubbed his chin.

CHAPTER 10

Maya gently put down the baby. He'd been gurgling happily for the past half hour or so, and looked ready for his nap. "Sleep, little baby," Maya sang softly as she watched her little brother with affection. She wondered how it would feel to have a baby of her own one day. First she would need to find a boy she would want to spend the rest of her life with. She thought about her boyfriend Mark Dean and wondered not for the first time if he fit the bill.

She knew all about high school sweethearts. How a relationship like that rarely stood the test of time. Only one more year and she was off to college. Would they still see each other? She was going to Washington University, where her dad taught, but Mark was still wavering. He didn't even know if he wanted to go to college. His dad ran a sawmill and was hoping his son would follow in his footsteps and take over the business. He didn't need a college degree to do that. In fact it would probably hamper him and his dad's business as he could step into the company right now, instead of having to wait four years before he did.

Tough decisions.

She looked up when Scott entered the room, a strange grin on his face.

"What's up, little brother?" she asked, glad for the respite. "Do they know who the dead guy is yet?"

"His name is Hot Gangster," said Scott, plunking himself down on the other bed.

She shot up. "Hot Gangster? No way!"

"Way," said Scott as he took out his phone. "Real name Donny Towns," he read, frowning, then looked up. "Though he registered at the motel under the name Adam Plauder. And get this. He booked a room with his ex-wife." He stared down at his phone again. "Wow. Hot Mama. Real name Christy Cadanet, though she registered as Christy Plauder when she booked the room."

"He was here with his ex? But why?"

She was fired up now. This was not what she'd expected from this sleepy little town or this sleepy little motel. "And what will Tracy Hall think? Or her father?"

"They're here," said Scott casually, and when she cried 'Omigod' he grinned. "Yeah. The receptionist—her name is Vikki Mammal if you can believe it—said Wilbur Hall was asking about Hot Gangster just before Ralph found him buried under a foot of snow. He said they were supposed to meet."

"They?"

"Wilbur, Tracy and Hot Gangster."

"Meet? Here? In the middle of nowhere? That doesn't make any sense."

"No, it doesn't, does it?" said Scott thoughtfully. "People like the Halls don't stay at places like the Gateway Lodge. So why would they meet all the way out here?"

"What do the police think?"

"No cops involved."

"No cops?"

He pointed to the window. "The blizzard, remember? They shoved Hot Gangster into the kitchen freezer and they'll probably only take him out again in three days, when the storm has blown over."

"They do have a strange way of doing things out here in the sticks," said Maya.

"I wanted to snap a shot of Hot Gangster but the manager caught me. Oh, and I told him Dad is a famous criminologist. So remember when he asks you, all right?"

Maya was shaking her head. "What have you gone and done now?"

☙

Dee had just put her foot on the first step of the stairs when the manager came running up to her and Tom. "Mr. and Mrs. Kelly! Can I have a moment of your time, please?"

If this was about the turd, Dee wasn't in the mood. She'd flushed that thing down the toilet ages ago and as far as she was concerned they had bigger fish to fry right now. Like how to deal with her son coming upon a dead body. She was thinking about what friend of a friend might know a good child psychologist to help Scott deal with the trauma.

"What is it?" asked Tom.

"I need your help, Professor Kelly," said the manager, glancing around nervously. "Can we..." He gestured in the direction of the reception desk. "Can we please step into my office for a moment?"

Reluctantly, Dee followed her husband and the manager. They stepped behind the reception desk and into a little office located there. The name on the door indicated this was the home of Vernon Haggis, Executive Manager, and the moment they were inside Vernon quickly closed the door and bade them to take a seat while he did the same.

He steepled his fingers on his blotter and stared at them for the space of ten seconds, then blurted out, "Your son told me about your achievements, Professor. Your reputation proceeds you. And it's at times like these that I sometimes think that the Lord does work in mysterious ways his wonders to perform." He cleared his throat. "I have a dead body in my freezer, Professor Kelly, and the police are unable to join us at this time to conduct an investigation into the poor man's death. I implore you—I beseech you... Can you take on the investigation until the police show up?"

Tom blinked a few times, and Dee pressed her lips together. "What did Scott tell you?" she asked.

"Well, that your husband is a brilliant criminologist, of course, and that his work led to the establishment of the Behavioral Science Unit at the FBI and even led to that wonderful television show that I'm afraid I haven't had the time to watch yet but which I'm sure is just wonderful and very complimentary of your work for our federal crime-fighting agency."

There was a pause in which Vernon smiled beatifically at Tom, Tom stared back dazedly at Vernon, and Dee silently cursed Scott for putting so much nonsense into this man's head. "Look, Mr. Haggis. I think we need to explain to you how—"

"I would be very happy to help you," Tom interjected.

She stared at her husband. Had he gone completely mad? Had the snow and the cold affected his mental faculties?

But before she could put these thoughts into words, Tom placed a hand over hers and squeezed it gently. "I'm only too happy to look into this case, Mr. Haggis," he said.

"Vernon, please," said Vernon, his face a thing of beauty as he suddenly radiated both relief and gratitude. "Oh, I can't thank you enough, Professor Kelly."

"Tom," said Tom.

"Tom," said Vernon, reaching across his desk to grasp Tom's hands and press them happily. "He's in the freezer," he said by way of changing the subject. "Care to have a look?"

CHAPTER 11

"What do you think you're doing?" hissed Dee as they set foot for the kitchen.

"Helping out this poor man by trying to solve a murder," said Tom.

"Are you out of your mind? You're not a criminologist! You're an economist!"

"I know what I am, thank you very much," said Tom. He couldn't help feeling Dee could be just a touch more supportive in this new venture they were about to embark on.

As it was, he'd always been something of an amateur sleuth. His favorite novels were mystery novels. His favorite TV shows were crime shows. And his favorite newspaper articles were accounts of murder and mayhem. True, he was an economics professor, and he was passionate about his profession. But he considered crime a hobby, and one he'd always hoped to bring to the next level. He enjoyed chatting with his criminologist colleagues and they invariably told him he had a crime fighter's mind tucked away inside an economist's body, whatever that meant.

And now here was the chance of a lifetime: the unique and wonderful opportunity to apply his keen analytic mind to a practical problem. A man had been killed. Someone had killed him. So who was it? How hard could it be to figure out the solution to the problem?

"What are the police going to say when they get here and find out you've been lying about who you are?" Dee continued as they followed behind Vernon Haggis, who was now walking with a distinct spring in his step, having secured the assistance of the great Professor Kelly. "And what is the university going to say when they hear you've been impersonating the founder of the FBI's Behavioral Science Unit!"

"I'll just tell them it's one big misunderstanding. I never said I was this person. Vernon simply misunderstood. And by then I will have caught the killer and everyone will be happy."

"*We* will have caught the killer!" she snapped.

He gave her a sideways look of confusion. "I don't understand."

"Do you really think I'm going to let you have all the fun? We're in this together, Professor Kelly, whether you like it or not!" Besides, she couldn't very well allow him to make an ass of himself now could she? Tom might be possessed of a brilliant mind, but he didn't know the first thing about catching killers. He was going to need all the help he could get.

"And here we are," said Vernon as he opened the door to the freezer with a flourish, like Aladdin opening the Cave of Wonders. He stepped aside and Tom and Dee stepped in.

It was pretty chilly, and as Dee's eyes adjusted to the relative darkness, and the slight fog that permeated the place, she saw that near the back wall a table had been set up, and on top of this table, a tarp had been placed. She pointed to the tarp. "Is that…"

Vernon, who'd stepped in after them, nodded. "That's Hot Gangster."

They approached the table and Vernon did the honors: he lifted the tarp, not unlike a coroner in the morgue would, and the face of Donny Towns appeared.

To Dee, the shock was less now, as she'd been face to face with the man before. But Tom's hand flew to his own face and he uttered a startled cry. "Oh, dear!" he said mutely.

A quick frown flitted across Vernon's features. "Surely this is not your first dead body, Professor Kelly?"

"Oh, no," said Tom, and produced a hoarse chuckle. "It's just that… he looks so familiar."

"That's because he's a celebrity," said Vernon, understanding Tom's sentiments exactly. "It's always a strange thing to see a dead celebrity. So familiar yet so unfamiliar, if you see what I mean."

Having dispensed with this little bit of philosophy, the executive manager of the Gateway Lodge tugged down the tarp and pointed to the man's chest, where the knife was stuck, pointing up like an extra body part. "I'm not an expert, but I'd say that's how he died."

"Do you recognize the knife?" asked Tom, his interest now piqued.

"It's one of ours," Vernon confirmed. "At least," he hastened to clarify, "It looks exactly like the kind of carving knives we use in this kitchen."

"Have you checked if one is missing?" asked Dee.

The manager smiled and pointed at her. "Good idea. I'll do that right now, shall I?"

And off he went, on a little trot, happy to be of the great Professor Kelly's assistance.

"How are we going to do this?" asked Dee. "We're not cops."

"How hard can it be?" said Tom. "I've read a ton of crime novels. You've watched a ton of crime shows. Together we can do this, honey." He gave her a reassuring smile. "We can crack this case."

She rolled her eyes, then noticed how cold her eyeballs felt. "It's freezing in here."

"Uh-huh," said Tom, who was now studying the body closely, impervious to the cold. He'd taken out those reading glasses again, and was studying Hot Gangster like he would study a book on some obscure economic theory. This was the Tom she knew: the brilliant academic who could focus so absolutely on something he lost all track of time and every sense of his surroundings. Maybe he was right. Maybe the qualities that made him a great economist would help him solve this case.

Or maybe the cops would eventually show up and throw them both in jail for tampering with evidence, obstruction of a police investigation, and impersonating the founder of the FBI's serial-killer unit, a unit, coincidentally, which had been founded when Tom was still in diapers and his first *Hardy Boys* novel was still beyond the grasp of his grubby little fingers.

CHAPTER 12

There seemed little they could learn from staring at the dead man's body. He looked peaceful in death, Tom thought, though what did he know? He'd never seen a dead body before—apart from the frog he'd dissected in middle school when he'd almost passed out. At least this time he was able to keep the contents of his stomach inside.

From experience Tom knew that there was a ton of evidence that could be gleaned here, and with experience he meant the 'ton of crime novels' he'd read in the forty-eight years of his existence, including the complete set of *Hardy Boys* novels his parents had gotten him as a kid and which, he now felt, had prepared him for the life of a sleuth. He'd even read a few *Nancy Drew* novels, stealing them from his sister when she wasn't looking.

The evidence, however, could only be gleaned by those funky CSI people, dressed up in their funky white suits, and using an array of funky high-tech equipment. There were hair and fiber and fingerprints and DNA and possibly a bunch of other stuff attached to the body of the late Donny

Towns that he couldn't even begin to fathom or harvest at this moment.

Too bad. He'd just have to depend on good old-fashioned detective work to compensate for his low-tech approach. At least the suspects weren't going anywhere. Like him and his family, they were stuck here in Middletown, at this crappy little motel.

The manager had returned and was holding a knife, waving it with visible glee.

"I found it—look, Professor. Exactly the same as the one used on Hot Gangster!"

Tom looked, and deduced that the manager was right. The knife he was waving did indeed look exactly the same as the one stuck inside Hot Gangster. "But is there one missing?" he asked, a gentle reminder of the original mission Dee had given the manager.

"Oh, right!" Vernon cried, and trotted off once more, happy to be of assistance.

Tom was rubbing his chin, like a real detective would, or at least a fictional one. "I wonder," he said.

"Wonder what?" said his wife of twenty years.

"If I'm Sherlock Holmes, what does that make you —and him?"

"Well, I'm Watson, obviously," said Dee.

"I don't think so. I think you're Irene Adler and Vernon is Watson."

Dee smiled. "You think I'm a femme fatale?"

He pulled her to him and kissed her sweetly on the lips. "Of course I do. You're *my* femme fatale."

"I could be your femme fatale *and* your Dr. Watson," she suggested, leaning in.

"True, true," he admitted, the proposition holding a certain appeal. "Then again, I've never met a more perfect Dr. Watson than Vernon Haggis. Have you?"

"He does fit the part to a T," said Dee, as they watched the manager hop to again, his face lit up with the glow of excitement.

"Eureka! Eureka, Professor!" he said, like some latter-day Archimedes. Tom saw, to his surprise, that the manager had brought along a hefty knife block. Vernon pointed at the block. "Look! Look, Professor!"

Tom looked, and so did Dee, and that's when he saw it: the full array of knives was present and accounted for, except for one. "Is that..."

"That's the one!" Vernon cried. "Has to be! The murder weapon, Professor! This is it!"

"Good work, Wa—I mean, Vernon," said Tom, patting the manager on the shoulder. Now they were getting somewhere. "So who had access to this kitchen of yours?"

The manager scrunched up his face. He was thinking. Hard. He hugged the knife block to his chest for good measure. Finally his face cleared. "Everybody."

"Everybody? What do you mean, everybody?"

Vernon shrugged. "I run a fairly standard-issue motel, Professor Kelly."

"Tom."

"Professor Tom. There's no high-end security measures or special access badges required to move around. I have a small staff of people who've been with me for years, and they move around freely, as do the guests. Basically anyone could have come in here and taken that knife before sticking it into Mr. Hot Gangster over here."

"No security cameras?"

"None."

"Mh," said Tom, once again stroking his chin. He'd never noticed it before, but the stroking seemed to stimulate his mental faculties, helping him think. It also looked cool.

"What do you think, Tom?" asked Dee.

He couldn't very well admit it in front of Vernon, but he had no clue what to think. If anyone and everyone had access to the kitchen, it was a little hard to pin down who might have done the dirty deed. Then he remembered what Hercule Poirot used to do. "Let's set up some interviews with potential suspects, shall we? Verify their whereabouts. Oh, and do you have a doctor on the premises?"

"A doctor? Aren't you feeling well, Professor Tom?"

"To examine the body," he said.

"But he's dead."

"Yes, I think we've established that."

"So what do we need a doctor for?"

Tom shrugged. "It's customary on these occasions to have a doctor present."

Vernon gave him a dubious look, then said, "Jim and Eden Grive are doctors. They're in 36C."

"Oh, we know Jim and Eden," said Dee. "We met when we checked in, remember, Tom?"

"I do," said Tom, well pleased. He liked the Grives. "Better get them down here ASAP, Vernon. They need to check the body. See if there's anything we might have missed."

Vernon was still skeptical, but his demeanor indicated that Tom was now the man in charge, and that he deferred to his superior crime-fighting genius.

"I'll get the Grives," he said as they walked out of the walk-in freezer. "So who do you want to interview first, Professor Tom?"

Tom thought about this for a moment, then said, "The ex-wife. Christy Cadanet."

"Consider it done," said Vernon ominously, closing the freezer.

As Vernon went about his business as Professor Tom's second-in-command, Dee said, "This is not how I imagined our family vacation to end, Tom."

"Me neither."

"I mean, do you really want to do this? We have the kids to think about. They might not like the idea of their parents snooping around like a bunch of wannabe amateur detectives."

"This was Scott's idea in the first place, remember? I'm sure they'll be fine with it. In fact," he added, wagging his finger like the professor he was, "they might be able to help."

CHAPTER 13

Scott was lying on the bed, playing Candy Crush on his phone, the stirring events of the morning long forgotten, when his parents finally returned. "Took you guys long enough," he grumbled. He was hungry—not just for food but for news about feeding times and storm updates.

"We've got you to thank for that, hot shot," said Dad.

Scott frowned, then remembered his brainwave from before and grinned. "He really believed that crap I fed him about you being a famous criminologist, huh?"

"Oh, he bought it hook, line and sinker, buddy," said Dad, taking a seat on the foot of the bed. "As a consequence you're looking at the lead investigator in the murder of Hot Gangster."

"Cool!" said Scott, putting down his phone and sitting up. "So did you catch the killer? Was it the wife? It's always the wife, right? Isn't that what the cops usually say?"

Dad was smiling, which put Scott's mind at ease. He'd half expected to get in trouble for saying that stuff to the manager. "I don't know yet, Scott. Mom and I have just begun."

"Mom and you? You're both doing this?"

"Sure. And what's more, we want you and Maya to help us out."

Scott's eyes grew wide. "You want us to help you solve this murder? Are you serious?"

"Dead serious," said Dad with a grin.

"You have got to be kidding," said Maya from her bed, where she'd been exchanging flirty text messages with her boyfriend. Probably lots of hearts and kisses and stuff. Yuck!

"We're not kidding," said Mom, who was checking the baby. "If we're going to do this we have to do this as a family. It can't just be your dad and I going off and doing a lot of poking around and talking to people while you kids are stuck in this room all day. We want you to poke around, too. See what you can find out. Maybe talk to other kids your age —make friends and find out what's been going on with this Hot Gangster and his wife."

"I can do that," said Scott, nodding excitedly. This was exactly the kind of thing he was happy to sign up for. Better than looking at a bunch of crappy monuments or visiting boring old museums with his grandparents and his cousins from hell. Although they'd been to the National Museum of the Air Force and he'd sat in one of those fighter jets and that had been pretty neat. He'd even seen an actual stealth fighter. But then his cousin Mike had given him a wedgie in front of a bunch of cute girls. Ugh. Talk about a juvenile hooligan.

"I don't know, Mom," said Maya. "We're not detectives. How are we going to get people to talk to us?"

"People love to talk, honey," said Mom. "Especially about something like this. You just make sure you pay attention. You'll be surprised how much you can find out by simply listening to people and paying attention."

"But aren't we going to get in trouble? I mean, when the

police finally show up and they take over the investigation? There must be laws against this kind of stuff, right?"

Scott looked at his father, who'd picked up his iPad and was fiddling with it. "Dad?" he asked. "We're not going to get in trouble with the cops, right?"

"Oh, of course not," said his father absentmindedly. "The cops will be happy—thrilled that we did them such a huge favor."

"I'm not so sure about that," Maya muttered, and when Scott looked over to his mother her expression seemed to mimic Maya's reservations.

"Listen to this," Dad said. "Hot Gangster was engaged to be married—the wedding was scheduled for next week in Arkansas, on the Hall family estate out there." He looked up. "So what were they all doing out here in this floppy little motel in Middletown?"

&.

Wilbur Hall was wringing his hands. He'd always read that people did that sometimes when under great stress, but he hadn't realized it was really a thing until now. So he was wringing his hands and pacing the floor of his crappy little room in this crappy little motel out in the sticks and cursing himself and the guy the world knew as Hot Gangster.

"Idiot!" he was muttering. "Nincompoop! I should have known this would happen."

"How could you know he was going to get himself killed, Dad?" asked his daughter, who was the picture of poise and grace, even under these terrible circumstances.

They should have been staying at a suite in the Hilton Cincinnati or the Hyatt Regency. They would have been in adjoining suites, with connecting doors, respecting his daughter and her future husband's privacy yet still connected if his little girl needed her old man's sage advice and company. Instead they were sharing a dingy room in a dingier motel!

"Did you know he was out here with his wife? His wife! The wife he walked out on!"

"I know, Dad. You only told me about a gazillion times already."

Tracy was lying on the bed, staring up at the ceiling, ostensibly not a care in the world. Wilbur knew better, though. He knew she was devastated by Donny's betrayal. "Maybe it's all for the best," Wilbur now said, still wringing his hands and tracing a rut in the carpet. "Imagine you married the guy and a week later it turns out he was still seeing his wife."

"Ex-wife," said Tracy, still lying motionless. She was clad in designer jeans and a yellow designer sweater, her blond hair spread out across the pillow. She looked so much like her mother these days that it made Wilbur's heart constrict when he looked at her.

"It seems to me Donny had a strange conception of the word ex, honey. And it also seems to me that the only reason he was interested in you was because of our standing."

She finally looked up at this, her beautiful eyes glittering. "You mean he only got involved with me for my money. That's what you're saying, right?"

He spread his arms. "The evidence seems to bear it out, Tracy."

"I don't believe you," said his daughter, and let her head fall back on her pillow.

"Why else would he be out here meeting Christy? And I'll bet she brought their baby along with her, too. It's obvious to me he was still in love with the woman—and he only divorced her so he could marry into our family and into our family fortune."

But Tracy was shaking her head. "Donny wasn't like that, Dad. He told me he left her. He told me he loved me. And I believed him."

And that was the problem with men like Donny, wasn't it? They were so charming they could make any woman fall for them—especially a vulnerable woman like Tracy. Which is why Wilbur had had the good sense to hire that private detective who'd taken a closer look at Donny's connections, his finances, criminal record, the works! And when it turned out Donny had booked a room at the Gateway Lodge, smack dab in the middle of nowhere, a week before the wedding, Wilbur had immediately flown out to confront his future son-in-law, convinced he was up to his old tricks again. Only Tracy had insisted she join her father. They hadn't even had the chance to meet Donny and find out what he was up to before the idiot turned up dead. And now here they were, right in the middle of a big, ugly mess!

He ground his teeth. "And here I figured he was meeting some drug dealer associate, or some other lowlife he owed a bunch of money to. Instead he was meeting his wife!"

"Ex-wife."

All things considered, they'd had a narrow escape, Wilbur now saw. One week more and that deceitful bastard would have married into his family and made Tracy his wife. Maybe it was all for the best. At least now Donny would never be able to break Tracy's heart with his shenanigans and his cheating. And if the police made a stink he'd hire the best lawyers he could find and get them both out of here the moment the weather cleared.

He stared out at the blizzard now fully expending its rage outside.

Three more days of weathering this storm. They should be able to manage.

CHAPTER 14

Samuel Kwiek threw up his hands. "I can't do this, Vernon!" he was screaming. "I have standards! If you make me do this I quit!"

"You can't quit," said Vernon soothingly. "There's a snowstorm blasting outside, I've got thirty guests to feed and I can't cook! You have lunch to prepare, Sam. So better get to it."

"There is a dead body in my freezer! Have you not seen the dead body, Vernon? *Alsjeblieft zeg!*"

Sam Kwiek was of Dutch descent, and from time to time, and especially when he was under a great deal of pressure, traces of his native language shone through.

"It's fine, Sam. I covered him up with a tarp. And I separated him from the rest of the food."

"The 'rest of the food?' He's not food, Vernon. He's a human being!"

"I know, I know. Look, what do you want me to do, huh? I can't leave him out here. He'll start to stink up the place. Trust me, the freezer is the best place for a dead body."

"You could have simply left him outside," said Sam, his

arms folded across his chest and brooding. "Why did you have to dig him out? He was fine where he was. In fact he could have been out there until springtime."

"I couldn't leave him out there—are you kidding me? A guest found him. I had to dig him out. If I left him they would have told the cops and they would have me for breakfast. No, this is the only way, Sam. And it's only for a couple of days. Three days and this will all be over." Vernon was practically on his knees now. Sam was the only cook he had —the others hadn't been able to come in because of the storm. If Sam went on strike, they'd have to eat sandwiches for the next three days. And he'd have to comp all the guests all of their stays.

"It's not just the dead body," said Sam. "It's also—I can't do this all by myself, Vernon. I'm a chef, not a line cook or a dishwasher. I need my people. I need my team!"

"And I'll get you your team," said Vernon. "I've already asked Vikki, and of course Beau and Alfa, and I'm getting Isobella and Adeola as well. They'll all be here soon." He checked his watch. "Soon," he repeated, more to himself than to the Dutch chef.

Sam looked aghast. "Isobella and Adeola? They're cleaners! They push a cleaning trolley!"

"I'm sure they can cook as well as clean."

"And Beau and Alfa. They're waiters! Not cooks!"

"I don't care, all right!" Vernon said, suddenly tired of this petty rebellion. "They're the only people I've got and they're going to have to put their best foot forward for the sake of the motel. Just... do the best you can," he added, softening when he saw the fierce expression on his chef's face. He just might throw down his chef's apron and walk out into the snowstorm never to be seen or heard from again, the crazy bastard. "I need you," he said therefore. "I can't do this without you, Sam. Pretty please?"

Sam finally relented, the fierceness bleeding out of his face. "All right," he said. "I'll cook for you, Vernon. But only because you're a good man. And you suffered a great loss when Audrey died. I wouldn't do this for just anyone but I'll do this for you. Just this once."

"Thanks, Sam," he said, relief making him almost giddy. If there was one thing he'd learned in his thirty years in the hospitality business it was that if you fed your guests well they forgave you pretty much everything. But if you didn't, you were dead meat. Which reminded him. "Did you see anyone in here this morning, Sam? Someone who wasn't supposed to be in here?"

Sam thought for a moment. "During breakfast, you mean? It was just me and Natalie this morning. No one else. And then of course Natalie had to go and return home before the storm hit and now I'm all alone in this great, big kitchen having to induct a bunch of rank amateurs into the art of my cuisine." He was frowning again, and Vernon thought it was probably a good idea to leave him to it. Poking the bear would only enrage him further.

So he left the kitchen to go in search of Sam's 'rank amateurs' and as he did so he thanked his lucky stars that at least he had professional help in the form of Professor Tom Kelly to deal with this murder business that had befallen this fine establishment. He was also reminded of his duties as Professor Tom's keen sidekick in setting up those all-important interviews. First things first, though. Lunch needed to be served, or else he'd have a regular mutiny on his hands, and he could not allow that to happen, nasty murder or no nasty murder.

CHAPTER 15

Dee knocked on the door of room 24B, half expecting there to be no answer. Tom had protested when she'd announced this initiative, claiming they needed to tackle Donny's widow—or ex-widow?—together as she was their most promising suspect. But Dee had argued that here was a woman whose husband had just been killed, and that probably no one had even bothered to tell her, seeing as they were all too busy dealing with the storm.

The door opened a crack and a teary face appeared. "Yes?" a tremulous voice asked.

"Mrs. Plauder? My name is Dee Kelly. I work with hotel management."

The crack widened and Dee saw that Donny's wife was thinner and paler than in the pictures she'd seen online. Her straw-colored hair was tied back into a messy bun and she was wearing jogging pants and a letter sweater that was entirely too big for her.

"Have you found Adam?" she asked now, dabbing at her nose with a tissue wad.

"Found Adam? You mean you reported him missing?"

The woman nodded tearfully. "This morning. I only went out to get some air and when I came back he was gone. I told the woman at the front desk and she said she would look into it. So have you? Looked into it?"

"Um… Can I come in?"

The woman opened the door and stepped back. The space was as cramped as Dee's own motel room, and her eyes immediately flitted to the window, under which Donny's body had been found. It was obvious Christy hadn't noticed all the digging that had gone on before, and Donny's body being carted away.

"The woman at the front desk. Do you remember her name?"

Christy frowned. "Daisy something? She was a big woman, with a round face."

That would explain things. Probably this Daisy had done the night shift, and had gone home in the morning without telling Vikki about Christy asking about her husband.

"The thing is, Mrs. Plauder… I'm afraid your husband… met with an accident."

"An accident? What do you mean?"

"I mean… I'm very sorry but your husband is dead, Mrs. Plauder."

The woman gulped, then broke into a loud wail. A second wail rose up from a baby cot that had been set up next to the bed. Immediately Dee hurried over, and saw a red-faced baby crying its heart out. It couldn't have been more than a few months. She picked up the baby and carried it over to its mother, placing it into Christy's arms.

"I'm so sorry," said Dee, feeling distinctly out of her depth here.

"I knew it!" Christy wailed, rocking back and forth,

hugging her baby. "I knew he wouldn't just walk out on me. What happened?"

"He… was murdered I'm afraid."

"Murdered!" Christy's wailing suddenly stopped and she seemed to focus. Seemingly automatically she put the baby to her chest. "What do you mean, murdered?"

"Stabbed. We found him at the bottom of this window." Dee pointed to the window in question.

Christy's eyes snapped to the window, then her jaw dropped. "You know? When I came back from my walk this morning the window was open. It was freezing in here. I just figured the cleaning lady must have left it open. To air out the room, you know. But…"

"It is possible that your husband was murdered right here and then pushed out of the window," said Dee, nodding.

Christy was frowning as she took all of this in. She swaddled up her baby and replaced it in the cot. "There's something I need to tell you, Mrs. Kelly."

"Yes?"

"My name isn't really Plauder. And Adam's name wasn't really Adam."

"I know who your husband was, Christy," said Dee gently. "And I also know you were divorced and he was about to get married to Tracy Hall."

Christy sat down again. She seemed more collected now. Calm. "If my ex-husband was murdered, why am I not talking to the police right now?"

"Because of the storm. They won't be able to get here until the storm blows over. In the meantime the manager of this motel is conducting a preliminary inquiry and he's asked me and my husband to assist him. Christy—what was Donny doing at the Gateway Lodge?"

Christy looked off, in the direction of the baby cot. "He called me last week. Said he was in the area and wanted to see the baby. She's his baby, too, you know, and he said he had every right to see her if he wanted to."

"And you didn't object?"

"No, I did not. I know you'll think this is crazy, but I never stopped loving him. Even after he… shacked up with that rich bitch."

"So why did you meet out here?"

"Because I didn't want my parents to know." She'd tilted up her chin. "They don't approve of Donny—never did—because of his past. And now, after the divorce, even less, of course."

"You live with your parents?"

She nodded. "Tough to be a single parent, Mrs. Kelly. My parents took me in but there was no way they were going to allow Donny to come and visit his little girl. So we decided to meet out here, where he could take his time to get to know his baby girl."

"And you checked in under a false name to…"

"To avoid people finding out, yeah. Not just my family, but the press, too. Donny's some kind of a celebrity now, you know. Press would have a field day if they knew he was visiting his ex-wife and his baby a week before his big fancy wedding." She pressed a hand to her face. "He said he was having second thoughts, too. That he'd gotten a little carried away and that he wasn't sure the big wedding was what he really wanted."

"You reconciled?"

"Maybe—well, I like to think we were getting there. He'd asked me to give him a second chance. And I told him I would have to think about it." She looked up. "He humiliated me, you know. In front of the whole world. Made me look like a real fool, didn't he?"

"I guess he did."

They were both silent for a moment, then Christy spoke

up. "I didn't do it, if that's what you think. I didn't throw my husband—or ex-husband—out of the window."

"Did anyone see you while you were out?"

"Plenty of people saw me. Not sure they'd remember, though. I'm not from around here, you know. Which is why we chose this place to begin with. Not to be recognized."

"And the reason Donny didn't come out with you…"

"Is because his face is a lot more famous than mine."

Dee nodded. She was inclined to believe Christy. Then again, what did she know? The woman had every reason to kill her husband after what he'd put her through. But did she?

※

The kitchen was humming along fine, Sam Kwiek focused and fully himself again, giving his assistants hell and creating the kind of lunch he was known for far and wide. Or at least to the fine folks of Middletown, Ohio. It wasn't just the guests who came for lunch. As the motel was located close to the freeway, they got a lot of tourists, too, and a fair bunch of locals who enjoyed Sam's cooking. He might not be the kind of chef whose creations would grace the cover of *Food & Wine* or *Taste of Home* but he was a fine cook nonetheless.

And he was just cutting up a thick slice of veal when he grasped in vain for his favorite carving knife. He frowned at the knife block, as if it had just dealt him a personal affront. "Where is my carving knife?" he bellowed around the kitchen, his voice easily drowning out the sizzling and broiling and clattering sounds that dominated the soundscape.

Beau came up, his apron a mess of egg yolk and tomato juice. "What knife, chef?"

"My best knife!" he screamed, pointing at the knife block located on top of the gleaming stainless steel table.

"Oh, that knife," said Beau. "Last time I saw that it was stuck in the chest of the dude that got murdered. You know, Hot Gangster?"

Sam gawked at his stand-in sous-chef. "They used *my* knife to murder someone?!" The way he said it made it sound like another personal affront. As if he didn't care that someone had been murdered but at least they shouldn't have had the gall to use *his* knife!

"Yeah, I guess so. If you want, it's still in the dude's chest. I can take it out if you like."

"Yes, please do," said Sam, making an irritable gesture with his right hand while he stirred the béchamel sauce with his left. "I need that knife. It's my knife," he added.

"Sure thing, boss," said Beau. "I'll just go and get that for you now."

As Sam watched the ex-waiter and newly appointed cook stalk off towards the freezer, Sam was shaking his head. What was it with people these days? Stealing knives to kill hot gangsters while they knew perfectly well this knife wasn't theirs to murder with? If they were going to go around and murder people they should very well buy their own knife.

Moments later, Beau returned, still dressed in that horribly filthy apron but sans knife.

"Well? Where's my knife?" Sam demanded.

Beau looked puzzled. "It's, um…"

"Oh, for goodness sakes I'll do it myself!" Sam roared, quick-tempered as always.

"No, chef, wait!" said Beau.

But too late. Sam was already yanking open the freezer door, cutting a straight path to the dead body that was a disgrace to everything the name Kwiek stood for, and dragging back the tarp. He paid scant attention to the man's appearance. He was used to being around dead bodies, though these usually were the bodies of the animals he carved up and served for breakfast, lunch or dinner. He cursed inwardly, and turned sharply when Beau joined him.

"Where is my knife!" he demanded once again, starting to feel like a parrot, having to repeat the same thing over and over again.

"Well, that's the thing, chef," said Beau. "It was right there—and now it's not."

"What do you mean it's not?!"

"It was sticking out of the dude's chest. And now it's not is all I'm saying."

He directed a furious look at the dead man, as if blaming him personally for absconding with his knife, then he threw his hands in the air and stalked out again.

"Incompetence!" he was shouting. "God how I hate incompetence!"

CHAPTER 16

Lunch was finally served and the few dozen guests of the Gateway Lodge all trooped into the dining room. After the kind of morning they'd had they were all starving. The Kellys found themselves seated at the same table as the Grives, and Tom was happy for this opportunity to have a little chat with Jim and Eden—this time in a professional capacity.

In spite of the fact that a man had been murdered, he felt that Vernon wasn't allocating enough time to the investigation and instead was more focused on running his motel. Then again, maybe that wasn't such a bad thing, as otherwise they would be starving right now.

"So what's all this I hear about you being some kind of top sleuth?" asked Jim.

Tom was pleasantly surprised. "Who told you—Vernon?"

"Yes, he did. He cornered me just before lunch. Said some dead body had been found and would I like to take a look at it. So I told him why the hell not?"

"And did you? Take a look at the dead body?" asked Scott, the topic clearly tickling his sense of excitement.

"Sure. In fact me and Eden did. Isn't that right, dear?"

"Yes, we did," said Eden, taking a dainty sip from her wine, then taking a bigger gulp.

"I didn't know you were doctors," said Dee.

"You never asked," quipped Jim. "We're both retired now, of course, but I guess it's true what they say. Once a doctor, always a doctor."

"At least when something happens to us we'll be in good hands," said Tom graciously.

Jim laughed. "At least you haven't dropped your pants to show me the suspicious hairy growth on your butt. How many times has that happened to us, Eden?"

"Oh, too many times to remember," said Eden with a throwaway gesture.

"Whenever you tell people you're a doctor they start rattling off a whole list of their ailments—big and small. I always tell them to make an appointment."

"So what about Hot Gangster?" asked Maya, who was as intrigued by this unexpected murder case as the rest of her family. "Did you get to see him?"

"Good-looking fellow," said Eden. "Well, he was," she added when her husband laughed.

Dee, who was feeding Baby Jacob, who was happily perched on his high stool, had to agree with Eden's professional opinion. Even though she wasn't a big fan of tattoos, the ones Donny Towns had were nicely done. And he had been a very handsome man. High cheekbones, cleft chin, remarkable blue eyes, thick, sexy lips. In life he'd been a stunner.

"I don't think that's what she was asking, dear," said Jim, wiping his lips with a napkin. "I mean, he was a good-looking fellow, no doubt about it. But was he murdered—that's the big question, isn't it? And how?"

"And?" asked Scott, on the edge of his seat now. "Did he jump or was he pushed?"

"He had a knife sticking out of his chest, Scott," said Maya. "Of course he was pushed. After he was stabbed."

Jim pursed his lips. "In my professional opinion the knife would have done the trick. Whether he did it to himself or not is hard to know for sure. Though from the angle it was stuck in the body I'd say he would have had a hard time doing that to himself." He held up his hands. "Of course I'm not a coroner or anything, so take this with a grain of salt."

"So was he killed?" asked Scott.

"Yes, he was," said Eden, taking another gulp of wine. "No doubt about it."

Just then, Vernon came walking up, looking distinctly nervous. "Professor Tom!" he said, bending down and tooting in Tom's ear. "Something terrible just happened!"

"What is it?" Tom asked, expecting the worst. Another dead body? More than one?

"The knife! It-it's gone!"

Tom sat up with a jerk. "Gone? What do you mean gone?"

"The chef wanted to take it out of the dead man—he needed it for carving—so Beau went to take it out—he said he was going to put it back when Chef was done with it—and that's when he saw that someone else had beaten him to it. The knife has vanished!"

"That's not good," said Jim, who'd overheard.

"That knife is evidence," said Tom, quite unnecessarily. "There could have been fingerprints on that knife—DNA traces—we need to find that knife, Vernon."

"I've had Beau search the kitchen top to bottom. It's nowhere to be found. Definitely missing."

"Oh, boy," said Scott, eyes shining with excitement. "The killer must have come back for the knife. To try and get rid of the evidence!"

"We should have locked that body up," said Tom. "Behind lock and key."

"We only have the one freezer," said Vernon, looking distinctly distraught.

They watched the manager hurry away, probably to put out another fire. The man had a lot on his plate right now, what with the storm and a motel full of guests and a dead man in his freezer and now this missing carving knife.

"So is it true you're some kind of super criminologist?" asked Jim, nudging Tom.

Tom, still thinking about the missing knife and what he could have done to protect it from whoever had stolen it, looked up. "Mh?"

"Vernon tells me you actually founded the FBI's Behavioral Science Unit. Which seems pretty tough seeing as the BSU was founded in 1972 and you don't strike me as a day over fifty."

"Forty-eight, actually," said Dee with a smile. "My husband didn't found anything, Jim. He's a Professor of Economics at the UW. Our son embellished the truth when he said that stuff about Tom being an ace crime fighter."

Jim and Eden both laughed heartily. "That's the funniest thing I ever heard!" said Jim.

"Amateur sleuths, huh?" asked Eden, gratefully accepting a slice of chocolate cake from Beau, who was bringing around dessert now. "I love it. So are you going to solve this case, Professor Tom?"

Tom shook his head. "I have no idea, Eden. Frankly I don't even know where to begin."

"We'll solve this case, Dad," said Scott, who seemed extremely confident. "And then the cops will have to give us a medal when we do."

"Well, I hope you manage, Scott," said Jim with a smile as he dug into his chocolate cake. "Murder is a very nasty business, even if the person who was murdered was a crook."

"Reformed crook," said Maya. "Well, it's true," she added when Jim laughed heartily. "He'd left that gang he was hanging out with and decided to turn his life around."

"What gang was that? The Crips or the Bloods?" asked Eden, who seemed to know a lot about criminal life.

"The Bloods, I think," said her husband. He was waving his coffee spoon. "You never really leave a gang, Maya," he told Tom's daughter. "We lived in New York all of our lives. Those kids keep getting pulled back in over and over again—until they end up dead in some alley or in some crack house. Mark my words, Hot Gangster was probably killed by some other gangster, hot or not. And whoever that gangster is, he's probably already legged it."

CHAPTER 17

"It's true, you know, Tom," said Dee as the Kellys had returned to their room for an impromptu meeting. "I mean, Jim is probably right. Whoever killed Donny Towns probably left right after he killed him."

"No, he did not," said Tom, a tiny smile playing about his lips. "And I'll tell you why."

Dee had placed Baby Jacob on the bed and watched as the little tyke folded his tiny fingers around her big finger and squeezed.

"I know, Dad!" cried Scott excitedly. "I know why the killer is still here!"

"Ugh. Isn't it obvious?" asked Maya. "He stole the knife, didn't he?"

"Exactly," said Tom, pointing at Maya like the college professor he was. He would probably have awarded her extra credit for that answer if he hadn't stopped himself. "The killer can't have left because he just stole the knife that must have contained incriminating evidence that could lead us—or the police—straight to him. Or her. Or them."

"So what if some careless cook took the knife, figuring he needed it?" asked Dee.

"In that case Vernon would have found it, wouldn't he?"

"What if said cook realized belatedly that he shouldn't have taken that knife and that now he was in big trouble so he simply hid it somewhere or even chucked it in the trash?"

That stumped the great detective, for his finger was hovering in the air and his mouth was open as if about to speak but the words or thoughts wouldn't come.

"Mom could be right, you know," said Maya, always the voice of reason.

"I like the other version better," said Scott. "Can't we decide—as a family—that the killer took it? That would be so much cooler. Cause if he didn't, and he skedaddled, this whole investigation is pretty much over before it started, right? And we don't want that."

"You mean you don't want that," said Maya.

"Hey, you like this as much as I do!"

"No, I don't. What, poking around in other people's lives? We're not cops, Scott."

"I talked to Christy Towns. Well, actually her name is Cadanet—even though to register at the motel she used the name Plauder. She said the only reason Donny was here was that he wanted to see the baby so they arranged to meet on neutral ground, since her parents wouldn't have approved."

"Donny's new wife probably wouldn't have approved either," said Maya.

"No, I'll bet she wouldn't. Anyway, Christy said she went for a walk with the baby just before breakfast and when she came back the window was open and Donny was nowhere to be found. So she figured he either had second thoughts or something happened to him. At any rate she told the front desk but then there was a shift change and then the storm hit and Christy's message never reached Vernon, or even

Vikki, I guess, so when I knocked at Christy's door that was the first she heard of her ex-husband's body having been found."

"But that's terrible!" said Maya, her hands flying to her face. "You mean she didn't know? Nobody told her what happened?"

"Apparently not."

"Vernon must have forgotten," said Tom. He took Dee's hand and squeezed it. "That was a very considerate thing to do, honey. How did she take the news?"

"Not well. It's obvious she still loved Donny, and she claimed he still loved her, and thought leaving her and the baby and getting involved with Tracy Hall was a big mistake."

"She said that?" asked Maya, stunned.

"And did you believe her?" asked Tom.

Dee nodded. "Yes, actually I did."

"We really need to talk to the Halls," said Tom. "To get a clear picture of what they were doing here. And then maybe we need to talk to Christy again. And find that knife, of course."

"How are we going to find that knife, Tom? That thing could be anywhere."

"We still need to find it. It was taken on our watch, and when the police finally get here they won't be happy about it."

"They can't blame us."

"Trust me, they will."

Tom was probably right. When the police arrived and they found one body minus the murder weapon, they wouldn't be happy about the Kelly family sticking their nose where it didn't belong. Nor would they be too happy with Vernon and his unorthodox sleuthing methods. At least Jim and Eden had confirmed the obvious: that Donny Towns was murdered. And they'd also provided another viewpoint: the possibility that Donny had been killed by a fellow gang member.

So now all they had to do was find a knife and a gang member and they were all set.

❧

Wilfred Dobosh shuffled up to the front desk and smiled nervously at the girl standing at attention. The poor thing looked dead on her feet. He remembered her from the day before, when she'd been in the same spot, looking a lot better than she did today.<>

"Have you been here all this time?" he asked. "That's just too much."

Vikki laughed, sounding a little raspy. "Oh, no. I went home yesterday and came back this morning, Mr. Dobosh. Otherwise I wouldn't be standing."

"Well, make sure you take care of yourself... Vikki," he said, reading her name tag. He pushed his thick glasses back up his bulbous nose. He was a short, stubby man in his late seventies, a Yankees cap on his head, and his eyesight wasn't as good as it once was. Then again, nothing about him was as good as it once had been. Ever since his wife Cecily died things had gone downhill. Not just his health but his mood, too, had worsened to a degree.

"What can I do for you, Mr. Dobosh?" asked Vikki pleasantly. She was a nice girl, Wilfred thought. Vivacious and kind. And she had a nice smile, too. "I just wanted to know if there's been a message for me."

"No message, I'm afraid. Are you expecting one?"

"Yeah. As a matter of fact I am." He hesitated, then decided to come right out with it. She did have one of those faces that one could trust. And after having been in the insurance business for over forty years he liked to think he could read faces like a book. "I was supposed to meet a fellow, you see. For a business transaction of sorts. He was going to leave a message at the desk. This is the only desk at this establishment, right?"

"It is. He could have been delayed by the storm," said Vikki.

"Yeah, he could have been," Wilfred said doubtfully, casting a quick glance through the door at the wintry landscape outside, where snow was swirling and the wind was howling. "Only he told me he'd arrive the night before."

"Do you have his name? I could see if he checked in yesterday."

"He gave me a name, but I doubt it's genuine." He lowered his voice. "You see, this business transaction of ours, it's strictly hush-hush. No real names involved whatsoever."

Vikki smiled an indulgent smile, probably thinking Wilfred was some old coot whose mind was starting to resemble Swiss cheese. "Just give me the name you have."

"Adam Plauder," said Wilfred, enunciating clearly. "I'll write it down for you if you want," he added when Vikki suddenly stiffened, her hands hovering over her keyboard.

"Did you say Adam Plauder?"

"That's right. So is he in?"

She gulped, which probably wasn't good.

"I'm afraid something happened to Mr. Plauder, Mr. Dobosh."

"Oh? What happened? Delayed, was he? Damn storm."

"No, actually he met with an accident this morning."

"An accident? You mean like a car accident?"

She stared at him, then seemed to shake herself. "I think you better talk to the manager, Mr. Dobosh."

CHAPTER 18

Wilfred was staring from the manager, a short guy with weird, bulging eyes, to the guy who introduced himself as Professor Tom Kelly, a handsome fellow with one of those professorial faces that exude erudition and old-world charm at the same time. If he'd lit up a pipe Wilfred wouldn't have been surprised.

"I don't get it. You're saying Adam Plauder was murdered? As in killed?"

"I'm afraid he was, Mr. Dobosh," said the manager. "Someone stabbed him and threw him out of the window."

"Or someone threw him out of his window and then stabbed him," said the professor. "Though that scenario is highly unlikely, of course." He cleared his throat. "You said something about a business transaction?"

He was still staring at the two men, not sure if he could trust them. They were ensconced inside the manager's tiny office, located right behind the front desk. Pictures of dogs papered the walls—probably this Vernon Haggis was something of a dog person—and a huge brass umbrella stand was located right next to the door. Behind the manager, a large portrait of a bulldog had been placed, its tongue lolling and its eyes protruding. And now that he looked at it, Wilfred thought there was a distinct resemblance between the manager and that bulldog.

"Look, I don't know how much I can tell you," he began.

"You're in good hands with Professor Tom," said the manager. "He's the person who founded the FBI's Behavioral Science Unit. They're the people who do all of that profiling, you see, and then they catch the bad guys—serial killers and such. He's a regular genius."

Professor Tom sat wincing slightly at this eulogy and Wilfred figured he did look the part of a genius criminologist. He relaxed a bit. "My wife died last year," he began.

"Uh-huh," said Professor Tom, now looking like a minor Sigmund Freud, prepared to dig in for a long and long-winded life story.

"Cecily hated my hobby. I collect baseball cards, you see."

"Baseball cards," said the manager.

"Got thousands of them. Rare ones and not so rare ones. Cecily always said I was wasting my time. That I could have spent all that money on a nice Caribbean cruise instead of that darned baseball card collection of mine. So I promised her that one day I'd take her on that cruise. But then she died, you see. And now I'm going to keep my promise. I'm going to take her on that cruise—or at least I'm going to take her urn and scatter her ashes to the four winds. And I'm selling my collection—something I should have done a long time ago."

He rubbed his face with his hands. He didn't have much longer. He could feel it in his aching bones. Soon he and Cecily would be together again. But first he had a promise to keep.

"You see, she was right, you know? All that time I spent on my collection? All that money? I should have spent on her. While we still had the time. While we could still travel.

And while we still had each other. Now she's gone, and I have my baseball cards to talk to. Only they're not so great company. Not as good as my Cecily was." His voice broke, and he inwardly cursed his sentimentality. "Look, I was here because Adam Plauder told me he could pay top dollar for the most precious card in my collection, all right? So when you tell me he's dead that comes as something of a surprise to me. And it kinda ruins my big plan."

"What's this card, Mr. Dobosh?" asked Professor Tom gently.

"Mickey Mantle," he said gruffly. "His 1952 Topps Major League card."

The professor seemed to swallow. "And how much was Plauder offering?"

"Fifty thousand smackeroos if you please. Enough to get me all the way to the Caribbean and back again." Not that he was planning on coming back if he could help it. But these wise guys didn't need to know that.

The professor had taken out his phone. Nice. Very polite. But then that was those damned millennials for you. Always glued to their phone and ignoring everything else.

"Where is this card now, Mr. Dobosh?" asked the manager.

"In your safe. At least I hope it's still in there."

"Let me check," said the manager. He stood and to Wilfred's surprise turned the bulldog portrait like a door. The damn thing operated on hinges. Behind it, a safe was built into the wall. The manager shifted a few dials, then swung the door open and retrieved an envelope from inside that had Wilfred's name on it. He shook its contents out on the desk and the Mickey Mantle card appeared, wrapped in plastic the way he bought it all those years ago. "It's still there," said the manager unnecessarily.

Wilfred stared at the card. "So the guy's dead, huh? So who's gonna pay for my cruise?"

"I think you will find that plenty of people want to pay for your cruise, Mr. Dobosh," said Professor Tom, looking up from his phone. He quickly checked the card and nodded sagely. "A card like this was sold at auction not so long ago for one million dollars."

Wilfred was staring at the professor, a shiver running up his aged spine. "A million dollars? You gotta be kidding!"

"I kid you not, sir," said the professor, smiling now as he showed him a picture on his phone. It was the exact same Mickey Mantle card that was lying on the desk blotter.

"Son of a turkey fart! That Plauder guy was trying to pull a fast one on me!"

"Yes, he was. He must have known the card was worth a great deal more than what he was offering for it, and he probably had a buyer waiting to take it off his hands."

"Well, in that case I'm glad he got it in the gizzard," said Wilfred before he could stop himself. "Well, I am!" he said when the manager lifted one of his thick brows, his eyes now practically popping out of his head as he studied that million-dollar baseball card. "Adam Plauder was a crook and a fraud and he was going to steal my money."

"His real name was Donny Towns," said the professor. "And he *was* a crook. A real one, I mean. He was also known as Hot Gangster."

"I don't care if he was hot or not, I'm just glad I escaped by the skin of my teeth."

"Better put that card back in the safe," the professor told the manager, who seemed reluctant to drag his eyes away from the face of Mickey Mantle and his blue ball cap, holding onto that yellow slugger and staring off into the middle distance, true victory on his mind.

"He looks like Tom Hanks," said the manager. "Doesn't he? In that baseball movie?"

"*A League of Their Own*," said the professor, smiling. "There's no crying in baseball!"

"That was a good movie," said the manager, picking up the card and returning it to the envelope.

"That doesn't look like no Tom Hanks," said Wilfred, indignant. "That's Mickey Mantle! All Mickey Mantle looks like is Mickey Mantle! He was the greatest athlete that ever lived—not some two-bit Hollywood actor!"

"Calm down, Mr. Dobosh," said Professor Kelly. "Vernon was just saying that there's a slight resemblance, that's all."

"Well, I don't like his mentality," said Wilfred. "Insinuating things about Mickey."

He'd gotten up from his seat and watched as the manager put the envelope back into the safe, closed it, then replaced the picture of that ugly bulldog in front of it. He pointed from the professor to the manager. "There are some things in life that are sacred, gentlemen. And Mickey Mantle is one of those things. A little bit of respect is all I ask."

"I certainly meant no disrespect, sir," said the manager. "Tom Hanks is a great actor and Mickey Mantle was a great athlete—no doubt about it."

Wilfred felt his blood pressure surge. He didn't care. "Don't you mention those two in the same sentence ever again, buddy. I'm not too old to slug you, you hear me?"

"There's absolutely no reason to slug me, sir," said the manager, starting to look uncomfortable. "And I do apologize for any aggravation I may have caused."

Wilfred sobered, took his Yankees baseball cap from his head and scratched his scalp. He suddenly felt a bit sheepish. "Anyhoo. I just wanted to thank you—especially you, Professor Tom Kelly. Do you really think I can sell that card for a million smackeroos?"

"If you play it smart you certainly could," said the professor.

He nodded his thanks, and stole a quick look at the manager. "Look, Tom Hanks is a great actor. In fact he's one of my favorites. So I'm sorry if I flew off the handle just then. I know you meant no disrespect, sir. It's just—what with my wife dying and all—and having to fly out here for this meeting with that douchebag that just died…" His voice trailed off and he suddenly felt distinctly weak-kneed.

The professor streaked forward and helped him to the chair and he sank down on it. He pointed to the bulldog portrait. "Tell me something—is that dog yours?"

The manager looked up at the portrait with a look of reverence. "Yes, she was. Lady was the greatest dog I ever had the honor of crossing paths with. She actually belonged to my wife."

"She died, did she?"

"Yes, she did. Both my wife and Lady passed away last year."

Wilfred grunted. "Looks like we've got something in common, you and I. We both lost our loved ones last year."

"It never gets any easier, does it?"

"No, sir, it does not."

"I actually started a dog shelter in Lady's honor. Hope to do some good in her name."

Wilfred patted the table. "You know what? If you help me sell that card to the highest bidder I'll give a nice fat donation to that animal shelter of yours."

"You would do that?" asked the manager, visibly touched.

"Yes, sir, I would. You really helped me out here, so now it's my turn to do you a good turn. And since Cecily and I were never blessed with kids, and my time here on God's green earth is running out, I figure I might as well do some good while I still can."

"Thank you, Mr. Dobosh," said the manager, clasping Wilfred's hands and shaking them heartily. "Thank you so much!"

"You're very welcome." He stared off into space for a moment, his mind far away. "Cecily loved dogs. She'll be smiling down at us right now, proud of her stubborn old hubby." Then he thought of something. "Did you ever catch this hot gangster's associate?"

Both men looked up, stunned. "What associate?"

"This Donny character wasn't in this by his lonesome. He was bringing an associate to the party. To determine the quality and to see if my card wasn't a fake." When the men didn't respond, he added, "Why, this partner may very well be the killer you boys are looking for!"

CHAPTER 19

Scott was alone in the room and frankly he was bored. In fact it wasn't too much to say he was bored stiff. He'd played all the video games imaginable. He'd chatted with his best bud Derek and told him the whole story about the murder and Derek was appropriately awed until he wasn't. And then he'd watched a few YouTube videos of a guy playing video games and making whacky comments while he played them and now he was bored.

He was lying on the bed wondering what he could do next when suddenly Ralph produced a plaintive howling sound. The dog had his paws up on the bed and was nudging Scott's side with his snout, then howled some more.

Scott scrabbled him behind the ears. "I'm sorry, Ralphie but we can't go out. There's a blizzard if you hadn't noticed. We'd be blown away if we went out now."

But when dogs have to go, they have to go, blizzard or no blizzard, and Ralph just kept on howling softly, and nudging Scott.

"Oh, now don't look at me like that," said Scott when Ralph gave him that sad dog look. The look that is capable of melting hearts and racking up Facebook likes and shares. "You know I'd take you out in a heartbeat but I can't. Mom told me not to set foot out of the motel cause if I do she'll kill me. If the blizzard doesn't kill me first, that is."

Ooooooooowhoooooo!

"Look, you're gonna get me in trouble here, Ralphie."

Ooooooooowhooo!

"I know. I know."

He scratched the dog behind the ears some more. And then he got an idea. One of those big, bright ideas he often got. The ones that did so much to enrich the lives of those around him—or turn them into a living hell, depending on how you looked at it.

First he needed to take stock: where were all the usual suspects? Maya had stepped out of the room to try and wrangle something from the vending machine downstairs in the lobby. Mom had taken Baby Jacob for a little walk up and down the hallways of the motel. Dad was probably still doing whatever he was doing with that funny little manager with the Danny DeVito face. So the coast was clear!

He jumped from the bed, eliciting an excited woof from Ralph, who pressed his snout into Scott's butt for good measure, trying to ease him along, then he slipped into his thick winter coat, put on his hat and gloves, and moved to the door.

The dog couldn't believe his good fortune. He stared at Scott for a moment, tongue lolling and disbelief etched on his canine features.

"Woof?" he barked.

"Yes, we're going. Come on, boy."

"Woof!" the dog barked, a happy bark this time. And then he was turning circles on the carpet, chasing his own tail, then jumped up against Scott, yapping happily.

"Quiet!" Scott admonished him. "We don't want anyone

to know we're going out, buddy." He pressed his hands on Ralph's fluffy head and looked deeply into those trusty brown eyes. "You understand? This is a secret mission, buddy boy. We have to be all stealthy and stuff, all right? So you be good and pad along nice and quiet, like."

Ralph must have sensed what his master expected, for he immediately turned quiet, sank down on his haunches and watched, ears pricked up as Scott carefully opened the door and peered out.

"The coast is clear," he announced a moment later, and then they were on their way, boy and dog moving along the hallway with measured speed, then down the stairs, through the lobby and in the direction of the dining room.

Scott was holding Ralph on his leash but he didn't even need to, as the Goldendoodle pranced happily along, staying by his side like the faithful canine companion he was. If Ralph was wondering why they didn't simply walk out the front door, like the last time they went out for a wee, he didn't give any indication.

Into the dining room they went, now wonderfully deserted, and then into the kitchen, where activities had likewise been suspended for the time being, the chef and his assistants on a well-deserved break.

Scott looked left—he looked right—and then he yanked open that freezer and stepped in.

"Yes, we're going on an adventure, Ralph," he said when the dog cocked his head and gave him a curious look.

It had been a while since Scott had last seen Hot Gangster in all his glory and he wasn't really looking forward to making the dead dude's acquaintance once again. But he was a member of the Kelly family, after all, and sleuthing was in his blood—or at least that's what he told himself.

So he made a beeline for the tarped-up dead gangster, drew back the cover and took a good long look at the corpse.

"So we meet again, Hot Gangster," he said under his breath, then took out his phone and took those snaps he'd meant to take last time but didn't have a chance to. After all, hadn't Derek expressed doubt about some aspects of Scott's story? These pics would set the record straight. And they would cement Scott's reputation as Penhurst High's coolest dude.

"Now it's your turn, buddy," he told Ralph. The dog looked up at him with his trusty eyes and Scott crouched down next to him. "Look, Ralph. There's a knife missing, all right? Someone took it. Most probably the killer. So we find the knife—we find the killer. Now use your nose to find the killer and I'll take you out into that freaky blizzard for as long as you want. That's the deal. Got it?"

It could have been Scott's imagination but he had the distinct impression the dog was smiling. At the very least he looked pretty excited about the prospect of finally going out there into that wintry landscape again. He gave a short woof and then put his paws up on the table and sniffed all over the dead guy. And then he was off—on a trot!

Scott grabbed hold of the leash and then he was following along, Ralph holding his nose to the ground as he smelled his way out of the freezer, through the kitchen and into the dining room.

They passed through the lobby, which was pretty much deserted except for a couple of old folks staring through the front door at the raging storm outside and shaking their heads, then it was up the stairs again, Ralph clearly on a roll —following some kind of trail.

Scott was afraid to speak—afraid to distract Ralph when he was obviously onto something. So he simply jogged along as fast as he could. They'd arrived on the second floor but still Ralph was going strong—now taking the second set of stairs and moving to the third floor, where the staff rooms were located, Scott knew.

The wallpaper was peeling here, and the wall sconces hung crooked and were made of cheap plastic instead of glass. The carpet was threadbare and worn out and when finally Ralph came to a full stop in front of a door, Scott's heart was hammering in his chest—not because of the frantic few minutes of action but from the sheer excitement of the chase.

"Is this it?" he asked, and Ralph gave a curt bark.

Scott swallowed, then applied his knuckles to the door and rapped it vigorously.

Moments later, the door opened and a fat man dressed in a wife beater appeared, his eyes half-lidded and his dark hair mussed. "Whaddya want?" he muttered, clearly not happy at being woken up by a kid with a dog.

But Ralph wasn't constrained by the niceties of social norms: he simply moved inside the room, dragging Scott along, and cut a straight path for a large wardrobe located next to the bed.

"Hey! What's the big idea?!" the guy cried.

"I'm so sorry, sir," said Scott. "But my dog is onto something here."

"You can't come barging in here like this! Who are you?"

"My name is Scott Kelly and this is Ralph," said Scott politely.

"Well... get lost, Scott Kelly," said the guy, scratching under his armpit.

The room was a mess: clothes strewn all over the place, and there was even a copy of a dirty magazine half hidden under the bed. "Is this your room?" asked Scott.

"It's just a spare room," said the guy. "For when members of staff are required to stay the night."

"You work in the kitchen, right?" asked Scott. He winced

a little at the strange odor that seemed to permeate the room, a mixture of sweat, bad breath, stinky feet and general lack of oxygen.

"That's right. I wash the dishes. What's it to you?" said the guy, watching Ralph with rising annoyance.

The dog was scrabbling at the wardrobe now.

"What's in there?" asked Scott.

"Nothing," said the guy, suddenly a little defensive.

"Can I take a look?" asked Scott, and stepped forward.

The guy cut him off, though. "I think you better get lost, kid. You and that dog of yours."

But Ralph wasn't taking no for an answer. His frantic scrabbling had managed to kick back the wardrobe door, which now swung open on the rebound and displayed a mess of clothes stuffed onto shelves and hanging from clothes hangers and a mirror attached to the inside of the door, an old picture of Pamela Anderson in *Baywatch* red taped up in a corner.

"Hey!" the guy cried, turning to look.

Ralph, the final obstacle removed, dove right into the wardrobe, and when he came back out, was holding a plastic bag between his teeth, then proudly trotted over to Scott and shoved the baggie into Scott's waiting hands. It was one of those Ziploc freezer bags.

Scott laughed when he saw what the baggie contained: a carving knife, blood caked to its blade.

"You stole this," he said, swinging the baggie in the guy's face. "You took this from the dead body in the freezer, didn't you?"

"That's mine," said the guy between gritted teeth, and tried to grab the knife from Scott's hands. "Give that back, you annoying little punk!"

"I'm a guest at this motel, so you better show me some respect," said Scott, keeping the knife out of the man's reach.

"Give it back!" the guy yelled and gave Scott a shove in the shoulder.

But Ralph wasn't going to stand idly by while his master was being manhandled. The moment Scott tumbled back the dog was on his hind legs, bearing his teeth and producing a menacing snarl, his front paws on the man's chest, and then he was barking furiously.

The guy held up his hands, clearly terrified. "Get him off me! Come on, man! Get him off!"

"Ralph, it's all right," said Scott. "I'm fine."

Ralph looked back to check and finally relented, dropping back down on all fours. He was still keeping an eye on the guy, though, ready to launch himself at him if Scott told him to.

"Good boy," said Scott. Then, to the guy: "Did you kill Hot Gangster?"

"Of course I didn't kill Hot Gangster!" said the dishwasher. He raked his fingers through his scraggly mane. "I just…" He shook his head. "Don't tell anyone, all right? I'll lose my job if you do. It's just that… they don't pay me very much in this dump. Chump change. And then that asshole chef—he's crazy. Keeps yelling at people. He's a terror to work for. So when I heard about Hot Gangster I figured I might take a couple pictures. Sell them to *TMZ* or the *National Enquirer*. But when I was snapping those shots I saw the knife and got a better idea."

"You were going to sell it," said Scott, who now saw the whole picture.

"Yeah." He deflated completely now, and sank down onto the bed. "I got a wife, kid, and a kid of my own on the way. You don't know how it is to have to scrape by like this. It's humiliating. So I thought if I took the knife I could sell it on eBay or something, you know. Make a few bucks. 'The knife that killed Hot Gangster' or something. People pay a lot of money for that stuff. And it's not as if he's going to miss it, you know. He's already dead."

"Yeah, but the police are going to miss some grade-A evidence," said Scott. "This knife is probably full of fingerprints of the killer and his DNA and stuff."

"Yeah, right," scoffed the dishwasher. "Who's stupid enough to leave their fingerprints and DNA on the murder weapon in this day and age? Hasn't everyone seen *CSI* by now? Or any of those cop shows? I'll bet whoever killed Hot Gangster used gloves."

"You still shouldn't have taken it," said Scott, gesturing with the knife. "It's evidence of a crime and stealing evidence is also a crime."

"Don't tell anyone, will you?" the guy repeated, pleading now. "I can't lose this job."

"I'll think about it," Scott promised. "Meanwhile I'm taking the knife."

The man made a throwaway gesture. "Do whatever you want," he muttered.

"You still have the pictures," said Scott. "I'll bet *TMZ* will pay a bundle for those. Give you a real sweet deal."

"Yeah, yeah, yeah. Get lost, kid. You kinda ruined my day."

Scott shrugged and walked out, Ralph on his heel, and closed the door behind him.

He then patted the dog and said, "Good job, buddy. You're an ace detective. A real ace."

Ralph barked happily, then made for the stairwell. Time for his reward: a nice stroll in a blizzard. Scott laughed as he trotted after the dog. And as they arrived in the lobby, he quickly made a little detour into the manager's office, stuck his head in the door to see if anyone was home, and when he saw his dad and the manager in there, chatting with some old dude, he gave his father a cheerful little wave.

"Here you go, Dad," he said, handing the clear plastic baggie to his father. "Found this upstairs. Catch you later."

And before his father was sufficiently recovered from his shock to say a word, he was off again. Promises to keep and dogs to walk and all that. Ralph definitely deserved it, and frankly Scott could do with some fresh air as well.

And since the front door was locked, he decided to step out through the kitchen entrance, which he'd noticed when he first paid a visit to Hot Gangster in his new lair, and for the next ten minutes or so he froze his tush off in the icy gale, his back plastered against the wall, the blizzard now at full steam, turning the world into a giant swirl of white.

Ralph did his business but even he didn't seem eager to venture out into this strange new world of ice and cold and quickly came prancing back, eager to return indoors.

And that's when Scott got another super-duper idea: Ralph had sniffed Hot Gangster for only a few seconds before leading Scott to the knife. What if he let Ralph sniff the knife? He'd probably lead them straight to the killer!

CHAPTER 20

Maya kicked the machine for good measure. Just what she needed: another crappy vending machine eating her money and refusing to disgorge the Snickers she'd selected.

"Can't get that thing to work, huh?" a voice spoke behind her.

She glanced back and saw she'd been joined by a strikingly pretty female. She immediately recognized her as Tracy Hall, Hot Gangster's wannabe wife.

"Yeah," she said. "I just wanted a Snickers but the machine decided otherwise."

"Let me handle that thing," said Tracy, and stepped up like a batter stepping up to the plate. She then gave the vending machine—an aged contraption by the looks of it—a hearty shove with the heel of her hand. When that didn't work, she grabbed the machine by the neck—or rather the sides—and gave it a vigorous shake.

For a moment a battle raged between woman and machine, its outcome uncertain, but then the machine finally gave up and disgorged the sweet treat, which fell into the bottom tray with a dull clunk.

"Hey!" said Maya, happily surprised. "You did it!"

"Experience," said Tracy with a smile.

Maya fished the Snickers bar from the tray and peeled back the wrapper. "Want a piece? You've earned it."

"Sure. Why not? My diet's ruined anyway." Tracy broke off a piece of the chocolaty treat and popped it into her mouth.

"You're Tracy, right? I thought I recognized you. You're, like, famous and stuff."

A vague smile crossed the young woman's lips. "I wasn't before, you know. I mean, before I met Donny. Now? I can't go anywhere without people recognizing me. It's driving my dad crazy."

"Must be tough," said Maya, commiserating as she took a bite from the candy bar.

"My dad always prided himself on being able to go through life without anyone knowing who he was—except of course for the people who needed to know. Now our faces have been plastered all over the covers of every gossip rag in the country—the world, even."

"You know, my brother found your boyfriend," said Maya, and realized how crazy and inconsiderate that sounded even as she said it. "I mean... I'm really sorry for your loss."

Tracy sobered. "Thanks. I heard a dog found him. Buried under a heap of snow?"

"Yeah, that's our family dog," said Maya. "My name is Maya, by the way. Maya Kelly." Just then, her brother and Ralph came bounding down the stairs for some reason. They didn't see her, though, and disappeared into the dining room.

Tracy, who'd followed her gaze, asked, "That the dog in question?"

"Yup. That was Ralphie. And my brother Scott. We're stuck here, just like you guys, I guess."

"We drove up here just to meet Donny, then got hit by that storm so now we're just waiting for it to blow over." She rolled her eyes. "And for the cops to arrive. I'm betting they'll want to have a word with my dad about Donny. And me, of course."

Maya wondered if she should say something about her family conducting an impromptu investigation but then decided against it. The fewer people who knew about their involvement the better. "Must be tough on you—losing your fiancé like that, I mean."

Tracy nodded and stared down at her feet for a moment. "Yeah, pretty tough," she said softly. "We were getting married next week. And now he's gone. Just like that. It hasn't really sunk in yet, you know. I mean, who would do this to him? I just don't get it."

"My mom talked to his ex-wife," said Maya, gauging Tracy's reaction. "Her and Donny were staying here under a false name. Pretty weird, huh?"

Tracy didn't look up, instead studying her feet as if she'd never seen them before. She was wearing pink Converse sneakers with yellow flowers. "His ex-wife?"

"Yeah. They booked a room as Adam and Christy Plauder. He was killed in that room, then shoved out of the window and buried under a foot of snow. If our dog hadn't sniffed him out he might have been down there until the spring."

Finally, Tracy looked up, and there was a tear in the young woman's eye. "I didn't know he was going to be here with his wife. Or ex-wife. We were supposed to meet Donny, you see. Dad and I had been to the opening of a new store, and Donny had flown out here to visit his family, so when he called and said to meet here and travel down to Cincinnati together so we could catch our flight, I just figured he couldn't wait to see me. And when he didn't show up when we arrived Dad asked the front desk. They told him he'd booked a room under an assumed name, and that he was staying here with another woman."

"I'm so sorry," said Maya. She could only imagine what Tracy must be feeling.

"Me too," said Tracy, a distinct quiver in her voice. "Dad thinks he must have been cheating on me with his ex-wife but I refuse to believe that. I think the only reason he was here was to see his daughter." She wiped away a tear. "Did you know he had a little girl? He'd never seen her before." She took a deep breath. "Do you want to know what I think?"

Maya nodded, a look of concern on her face. She felt for this woman.

"I think he arranged to meet us because he wanted to make peace with his ex-wife, and introduce her to me and my father. And introduce his baby girl, too. I don't know what he expected. Maybe for all of us to hold hands and sing Kumbaya. Or for me and Christy to fall into each other's arms and become BFFs for life. Donny was a dreamer. He wanted all of us to get along. He hated to disappoint people and he knew he broke Christy's heart when he left her. So this was probably his way of atonement or something. At any rate, something happened and now he's dead, so whatever he was planning didn't work out."

"Do you think his ex-wife killed him?"

Tracy arched an eyebrow. "You said he was killed in her room?"

"The room he booked for the two of them, yes."

"And where was Christy when this happened?"

"She told my mom she was out—going for a stroll with the baby."

Tracy scoffed. "In this weather? No mother would take her baby for a stroll in a blizzard."

"But why would she kill him? He's still the father of her baby."

Tracy fixed her with an intense look. "She hated him, Maya. She told him she wished he were dead. And she also told him that if he ever came near her or the baby she'd kill him herself."

CHAPTER 21

Dee was walking up and down the hallway, cradling Jacob and gently rocking him against her chest. He'd been crying up a storm right after lunch, but now he'd finally fallen asleep and was quiet. She glanced at his cherubic little face and felt her heart swell with love and affection. Even though Jacob had been adopted, he felt as if he were hers all the way.

When she'd lost the ability to conceive almost two years ago now, she'd tumbled into a deep depression. The operation that had put a stop to her and Tom's dream of having another baby had been the most devastating thing that ever happened to her. And that dark time would have broken her, too, if Tom hadn't managed to magically arrange the adoption of this precious baby boy. The arrival of Jacob had dragged her out of her depression and had ushered in a new era for the entire family. An era of hope and love and laughter.

She softly hummed a little tune as she continued to stalk the hallway. Suddenly she noticed a man staring at her. He was a thickset man with a gray buzzcut and a black little

Hitler mustache. His brows were so thick and beetling they practically obscured his glittering little eyes. All in all not exactly a portrait of beauty, she thought. And then she recognized him. This was none other than Wilbur Hall, founder of the Hallmart empire.

"Sweet baby," he growled, looking as if he were one of those people who liked to eat babies for breakfast.

"He's sweet now," said Dee. "But you should have seen him half an hour ago. He was trying to break the world record for the longest temper tantrum in history."

The man was standing in the doorway of what Dee assumed was his room. He was leaning against the frame, his hand fiddling with something in his pocket. He followed her eyes and took out the object he was fiddling with. It turned out to be a vape.

Square in shape and pink in color, it didn't look like it belonged to him. He must have realized this, for he said, a little sheepishly, "My daughter bought it for me. Normally I smoke cigars, but she's been trying to whip me into shape for the wedding and she thought this little doohickey would be better for my health. And it doesn't stink up everything I come into contact with. Her words," he muttered mutely. Then, as if realizing his social faux-pas, he quickly added, "Oh, excuse me. You must think I'm the world's most uncouth ass. My name is Wilbur Hall. My daughter is Tracy. You may have heard of her. She was set to get married next week to a fellow called—"

"Hot Gangster. Yes, I've heard about the wedding," said Dee.

"Wedding's off," grunted the tycoon, staring off. "Groom got himself killed. Terrible business. Just terrible."

"My husband's actually investigating your future son-in-law's death," said Dee. "And I'm helping him."

"Is that a fact?" asked the man, visibly wondering who on

earth would want to volunteer for a fool scheme like that. "He a cop?"

"He's a professor at the University of Washington up in Seattle, where we live," she explained. She wasn't going to tell this little man her husband was a criminologist but if he inferred from her words that he was she wasn't going to set the record straight either.

"Smart guy, huh? I like that. People who get the job done. Use their little gray cells. So what has he found? Who did it? Who does he reckon killed Donny?"

"He's still in the preliminary stages of the investigation," said Dee, remembering a phrase she'd once heard on one of those cop shows she liked so much. It could have been *Law & Order* or it could have been *NCIS*, she wasn't sure. It sounded pretty neat, though, and Wilbur Hall seemed to agree, for he nodded emphatically.

"You need to have those preliminary stages, Mrs…"

"Oh, I'm sorry. Dee. Dee Kelly. And my husband is Tom. In fact he was hoping to have a little chat with you and your daughter if that's all right."

"Well, we're chatting now, aren't we, Mrs. Kelly?" said the man gruffly. "What do you want to know?"

She hoisted the baby a little higher. He was getting heavy. "You and Donny were meeting up here at the motel? Is that right?"

"That's right. He told us to meet him here. No idea why. Seemed like a good idea at the time. He having gone home to visit his family—they're from around these parts."

"Middletown?"

"Springfield. And since we were down in Hamilton—opening a new hypermarket out there—we decided to fly out of Cincinnati together. Middletown seemed as good a place as any to meet up. Though why he picked this crummy little motel beats me. Or at least it did until I heard he booked a room with his ex-wife—woman by the name of Christy Cadanet."

"You think he wanted you and your daughter to meet his ex-wife?"

"Her and the baby," he grumbled. "Just before he left his wife he fathered a baby with the woman." He was scowling now. "Never liked the fellow. No need to deny it. No big secret. Didn't like him and didn't like Tracy getting married to him. Gangster."

"So who do you think killed him, Mr. Hall?"

"Ex-wife, of course. Must have hated him for dragging her all the way out here to meet his new wife and his new father-in-law. Hated him for leaving her with a newborn."

"I talked to Christy, actually."

"You did, did you?" he grunted, his scowl deepening as if he didn't approve.

"She doesn't strike me as a murderess."

"Very few people do, Mrs. Kelly." He drew himself up. "Let me give you a little trade secret. I've interviewed plenty of people over the years. Managers. CEOs. CFOs. What have you. They all come across as the most competent people you'll ever hope to meet, fulfilling your wildest expectations and then some. A company president's dream." His glowered. "The moment they're on the job, and think you're not looking, they let their guard down and that's when the real person comes out. And nine times out of ten it's ugly, Mrs. Kelly. Real ugly. Embezzlement, fraud, sexual harassment, power trips, incompetence, wastefulness, you name it, I've seen it. So forgive me if I don't believe Christy Cadanet's sob stories."

"She says she was out when her ex-husband was killed."

"Check her alibi. Check the time frame. Do your job," Hall snarled, emphasizing his words by pointing a stubby finger at the palm of his hand. "She's lying, now you catch her."

And with these words, and clearly feeling he'd said enough, he slammed the door.

Dee stared at the closed door for a moment, wondering if he was right. Had Christy been lying to her? It wasn't hard to find out. Someone must have seen her leave the motel. And someone must have seen her return. Only problem was: they didn't know when her husband was murdered, exactly, so there was no way to properly establish Christy's alibi.

It was at times like these, Dee thought as she returned to her room, that it would have been nice to have a real cop present, who actually knew what the heck he was doing.

CHAPTER 22

Tom was leaning over the desk, watching on as Vernon and Vikki went through the register, one name at a time.

"He must be in here," Vernon said, mopping his brow with his sleeve as he nervously tapped the keys. "He probably got here around the same time his associate arrived."

"But how do we know it's him, Mr. Haggis?" asked Vikki, her pale face a testament to her distress. "Over thirty guests are currently staying at the motel. It could be any one of them."

"I'll know him when I see him," Vernon assured her. "These gangsters all look alike. His picture probably resembles a mug shot."

One by one, he brought up the names of the motel guests, while Vikki dug out the copies of the picture IDs the motel required its guests to produce when checking in.

"Did Donny really have a driver's license in the name of Adam Plauder?" Tom asked now.

Vikki nodded. "Probably a fake. He also had a credit card in the same name, though. No idea how that works."

"He paid cash, right?"

"Uh-huh."

"Did you check the credit card to see if it was valid?"

She winced a little. "Wasn't me that checked him in, Professor. That was Daisy."

"If that credit card was a fake, like the ID, it should have been refused."

"Here," said Vernon. "Check this one. Prescott Nutt. If that's not a fake name I'll eat my hat."

"You don't have a hat, Mr. Haggis," said Vikki with a giggle as she dug into the pile of IDs, mostly driver's licenses. "Oh, here he is. Prescott Nutt." She frowned at the document. "He doesn't look like a criminal. Professor? What do you think?"

Tom took the piece of paper and studied the face of a bespectacled man with a long face and the kind of dazed look one often sees on these official government documents. "I don't know," he said finally. "He could be a criminal or he could be the governor of the State of Ohio."

Vikki giggled again. "That's not the governor, Professor. Our governor is a former *Fox News* reporter, remember?"

"Aren't they all?" Tom said, still frowning at the picture of Mr. Nutt. Then he had an idea. "Let's ask Christy. She must have met this guy, right? Or at least seen him before, if he's a known associate of Donny's." And then he made an executive decision. He gathered up the pile of documents. "I'm off to see Christy," he said, and started for the staircase.

"Ooh, me too!" said Vikki, quickly joining him.

"And me," said Vernon. "This is still my motel, Professor. And my investigation. So if anyone should be interviewing potential suspects about other potential suspects it's me."

"Good point," Tom had to admit, and then they were ascending that staircase.

Vikki was humming something under her breath, and it sounded a lot like 'We're off to see the Wizard.'

CHAPTER 23

Dee looked up when first Scott then Maya walked into the room.

"Where have you guys been?" she asked.

"Oh, I just happened to find the murder weapon," said Scott smugly as he unleashed Ralph and jumped onto his bed. "Well, actually Ralph found the murder weapon. I confiscated it from the dude who stole it."

"You found the knife?" asked Maya, her jaw dropping.

"Yes, I did," said Scott, casually studying his fingernails.

"But how?" asked Dee. "And why did you take Ralph?"

"He had to wee-wee," said Scott, now supporting himself on his elbows as he prepared to launch into his tale of derring-do. "But then I had the most brilliant idea. I told him he could have his wee-wee but first he needed to do me a solid."

"You tortured our poor dog?" asked Maya.

Scott frowned. "I did not torture him. He loved every minute of it. In fact I think Ralph has got what it takes to be a police dog one day." Ralph, who must have sensed he was the center of attention, hopped up on the bed and plunked himself down next to Scott.

"So where was it?" asked Dee. "Where did you find the knife?"

"Some loser dishwasher who stole it so he could sell it on eBay. He also took a ton of pictures to sell to *TMZ* so we're going to see some 'Breaking News' soon on your favorite website, sister dear."

"*TMZ* is so not my favorite site," said Maya.

"That's right. I forgot. *Seventeen Magazine* is your all-time fav."

"You wish," she said, rolling her eyes.

"So where is the knife now?" asked Dee.

"Gave it to Dad," said Scott, picking up his phone.

"I talked to Tracy Hall," said Maya, and Scott put his phone back down. She smiled when all eyes now turned to her. Even Ralph was eyeing her closely.

"Tracy Hall as in the Hallmart heir?" asked Scott, duly impressed. "The richest girl in the country?"

"Yup. I shared a Snickers with her. She's super cool. Very down to earth for a celebrity."

"She's not really a celebrity," said Dee. "She just happens to have a very wealthy dad and a famous—or infamous—boyfriend."

"Who's now famously dead," said Scott, with a touch of callousness Dee did not like.

"Please show some respect for the dead, Scott," Dee said.

"Sorry, Mom," he muttered.

"So what did Tracy Hall say?" Dee asked.

"Did you ask how many billions she's got?" said Scott. "Or what car she drives? I'll bet she drives a Lambo. If I had a couple billion in my bank account I'd def get a Lambo."

Maya ignored her brother. "She reckons Donny told her to meet him here so he could introduce her to Christy and the baby. Donny must have wanted to have one of those big reconciliation scenes before he got married again. Though if you ask me he also wanted his father-in-law to give some money to Christy so she could take good care of her new baby."

"She said that?" asked Dee, frowning. Tracy's words confirmed her father's story. Though that last part about Wilbur Hall giving money to his future son-in-law's ex-wife was probably wishful thinking on Maya's part, for Wilbur had not proven himself a big fan of Christy's. On the contrary. "So who does she think killed Donny?"

"Christy," said Maya decidedly. "She even told me that Christy once told Donny that she would kill him if she ever saw him again or if he came near her or the baby."

"Wow," said Scott.

"And I think she's right. Christy is the perfect suspect." She ticked off her fingers. "He was killed right there in their room. He cheated on her with a billionaire's daughter even though they were high school sweethearts and had been together since they were sixteen. Fame had made him weird and distant."

"You got that from *TMZ*," said Scott with a smirk.

"For your information, I got that from *Cosmo*, and it's true. Donny had changed since he became Mr. Hot Gangster. He was hanging with his new rich friends and ignoring the woman who'd supported him all those years, even when he was in jail."

"What was he in jail for?" asked Dee.

"Possession of a firearm and grand theft," said Maya, who seemed to have memorized Donny's entire life history. She continued with the ticking off on her fingers. "So he left her for another woman—younger and prettier and richer—but not before he got Christy pregnant and left her to deliver the baby all by herself, not even visiting her in the hospital." She cocked her head. "I mean, if I were Christy I might have killed him, too."

"So you think she lured him over here to the Gateway Lodge and then killed him?" said Dee. "That doesn't seem right. She must have known she'd be the prime suspect."

"She didn't care! All she wanted was revenge."

Dee thought about this. Christy had told her Donny regretted his decision to leave her and hook up with Tracy Hall. How the upcoming wedding was a mistake. And how he wanted to be with Christy and his new baby. So why would she kill him if that was true? Unless she'd lied to Dee, like Wilbur Hall had indicated. She needed to talk to Christy again. And this time she would take Jacob along. Tough for a new mother to lie to the face of a fellow new mother. At least that was what she hoped. Or maybe she was just being naive.

CHAPTER 24

"Where did you put the knife?" asked Tom as he knocked on Christy Cadanet's door.

"In the safe, where it's safe," said Vernon.

"Was that blood on the knife, Mr. Haggis?" asked Vikki.

"Yes, it was, Vikki."

"Omigod," said Vikki, eyes shiny.

Then the door opened and Christy appeared. Or at least Tom thought it was Christy. He hadn't had the pleasure of talking to her yet—that had been Dee's prerogative. "Mrs. Plauder?" he asked.

Christy's eyes flickered across the faces of the three people standing before her. "I thought you'd never come," she said. "I called this in hours ago."

They stepped into the room and Tom's eyes immediately were drawn to the window where the fateful incident had taken place, then to the spot where Donny had breathed his last few breaths.

"It's in there," Christy told Tom. Without waiting for a reply, she strode into the bathroom.

"What's in there?" asked Tom, following her.

She laughed a hacking laugh. "Funny." She pointed at the boiler. "Please fix it. I need hot water for my baby." Then she walked out again and closed the door, but not before snapping, "And don't come out before it's fixed, you hear me?" And slammed the door.

Tom stared at the boiler. It was one of those great mysteries of life how those things operated, exactly. He himself had never managed to make the boilers in his own apartment and later his house, tick, and he held out very little hope that he'd be able to bring this particular boiler back from the dead either.

So he tapped the door gently. "Um, Mrs. Plauder? I'm not—"

The door was yanked open again, and Tom found himself staring into the smiling face of Vikki Mammal. "We straightened it out, Professor. You can come out now."

"I'm not the plumber, Mrs. Plauder," said Tom.

"You look like a plumber," Christy insisted, then turned to Vernon. "So where is the plumber? I need the plumber. That boiler is busted. I can't give the baby a bath in ice water, you know. It's a health hazard. How would you feel if you rented a room without hot water?"

Vernon was nodding even as he took out his phone. "I'll have this fixed in no time, Mrs. Plauder. And please accept my deepest apologies. The Gateway Lodge is a fine motel and this is not the kind of thing we like to subject our clients to." He made a slight bow and then started to bark into his phone, momentarily removing himself from the conversation.

"Mr. Haggis is a can-do kind of person, Mrs. Plauder," said Vikki. "He'll have that boiler of yours fixed in a jiffy."

"It's the least he can do. First my husband gets knifed down and now my boiler is busted. This motel is really doing its best to break me."

"Mrs. Plauder—we know your real name is Cadanet," said Tom.

"Of course you do," said Christy, eyeing him nastily, as if she hadn't forgiven him for not being a plumber.

"We're here to ask you a few questions about your ex-husband," said Tom. "We would like you to take a look at some pictures for us. See if you can identify your husband's associate. The man he was here to meet?" he added when she stared at him dumbly.

"He was here to meet me," she said, folding her arms across her chest.

"We have reason to believe he was also here to meet an associate and buy a baseball card from a man named Wilfred Dobosh."

"What are you talking about?" She was starting to lose her temper again.

Tom smiled as ingratiating a smile as he could muster. It was the smile he'd perfected when dealing with the irate parents of students who'd failed to pass an exam. "Mr. Dobosh just explained the whole thing to us. He is a baseball card collector and has in his possession a rare card that your husband expressed an interest in. Which is why he arranged to meet him here so he could take a look at the card and buy it from him—along with his associate."

"What's all this about an associate!" Christy now yelled. "Who are you?"

"My name is Tom Kelly. I have taken it upon myself to run a discreet inquiry into the death of your ex-husband."

Her eyes were shooting sheets of flame across the room, and Tom was starting to feel distinctly ill at ease. No irate parents had ever looked at him quite like this.

"How much?" Christy demanded.

"Pardon me?"

"How much was Donny going to pay this Mr. Hogwash?"

"Dobosh. They arranged a payment of fifty thousand dollars."

Christy blinked, then her lips tightened. "That no-good piece of lying skunk!"

"I can assure you that Mr. Dobosh wasn't lying when he told—"

"Not him—Donny! He told me he wanted to meet me because he wanted to get back together again! That he wanted to blow off the wedding and wanted to come back to me! And all this time he was fixing things to buy a frickin' baseball card?" She was flapping her arms up and down like a chicken now. Her screaming awoke her baby, who opened her throat and started wailing like a fire alarm.

Meanwhile Vernon had returned to the room, the same man in his wake who'd carried Donny's body from his snowy grave and into the freezer.

"This is Ravi," said Vernon. "He'll fix your boiler, Mrs. Cadanet."

"Oh, screw the boiler!" Christy screamed, picking up her baby.

"I'll be in there," said Ravi with a grin as he quickly moved to the bathroom, a toolkit in hand.

"What's wrong?" asked Vernon.

"Professor Tom just told her about the baseball card," said Vikki quietly.

"Did you know about that, Mrs. Cadanet?" asked Vernon. "That your ex-husband was trying to swindle a pensioner out of an extremely valuable Mickey Mantle card?"

"He just told me," Christy said with a sweep of her arm in Tom's direction.

"That was not a very nice thing to do, Mrs. Cadanet," Vernon continued. "He was probably going to split that million dollars with an associate, wasn't he? So did you know—"

Christy's head snapped up. "Million dollars! Nutty professor over here just said fifty thousand!"

"Well, your ex-husband offered Mr. Dobosh fifty thousand for the card, even though he must have known full well that this card was worth at least a million, a fact of which Mr. Dobosh wasn't apprised and therefore—"

Christy was bug-eyed now. "Mothersmucker!"

"Mrs. Cadanet, please," said Tom.

"Son of a bucket!"

Tom cleared his throat.

"Shit on a stick!"

"Mrs. Cadanet," said Vernon. "Can I call you Christy?"

"Barbra Streisand!"

Vikki laughed, but when Christy turned on her with a furious expression in her eyes, she quickly muttered an apology.

"All this time he was out here to cheat some pensioner out of his money? Gah! He told me he'd changed his ways. Found religion. Babbled on and on about redemption. Begged me to give him a second chance." She shook her head. "Holy crap am I dumb."

"I'm so sorry, Christy," said Tom.

"Oh, go lick a duck," she said viciously, and turned away, rocking her baby, who was still wailing up a storm, no doubt feeling the strain from being so rudely awakened.

Tom looked at Vernon. Vernon looked at Vikki. Vikki looked at Tom. The three of them looked at Christy, still staring out the window. Tom was wondering how to bring the conversation back around to Donny's known associates but was momentarily at a loss.

Just then, the door to the bathroom opened and the handyman stepped out. "Boiler's all set, ma'am," he muttered, his eyes bright and merry, then quickly stalked off in the direction of the door and was gone. And in from the same door came Dee, cradling Jacob.

She seemed surprised to find a room full of people. Tom was even more surprised, though, but immediately saw what a great opportunity this was. If anyone could talk a woman with a baby down from the proverbial ledge it was another woman with a baby.

He gestured to Dee to come in and so she did. He then gestured frantically to Christy, her back still turned, then gestured just as frantically to the stack of driver's licenses in his hand and handed them to Dee.

She frowned down at them, then frowned at Tom, then frowned at Vernon, who stood rocking back on his heels, his hands locked behind his back, and Vikki, who was chewing her bottom lip. It was, as any general would have readily agreed, an impasse.

"One of these men is Donny's associate," whispered Tom, pointing at the IDs. "The reason they were at the Gateway Lodge was to swindle a pensioner out of a very valuable baseball card. Donny had offered fifty thousand for a card worth at least a million."

Dee's eyes widened. "No shit."

"Oh, will you two stop whispering," said Christy, turning. "I can hear every word."

"I'm so, so sorry," said Dee.

"My husband was not a very nice man," said Christy, a sad look in her eyes now. She looked up and when she saw Dee cradling Jacob, a mirror image of herself, she seemed to galvanize herself. "So you think he was killed over some stupid baseball card?"

"Yes, I do," said Tom.

Christy hesitated, then held out her free hand. "Let me take a look at those."

"Let me hold her for a moment," Dee suggested.

Christy handed over the baby and the moment she did, the wailing stopped.

Donny's ex-wife quickly flipped through the stack. "No, no, no, no," she muttered as she went along. Then suddenly she paused. "I know him. He was at the trial. He and Donny were in the same gang."

Tom, Vernon and Vikki drew closer and Tom saw that she was pointing at the picture of a square-faced man with a cleft chin, a handlebar mustache and deep-set eyes. The driver's license indicated his name was Ernie Saddling.

"That's not his real name," Christy said, confirming Tom's suspicions. "I don't remember his last name but Donny called him Marco. They were friends."

"So you met?"

"I never 'met' any of Donny's friends. I saw them at his trial. When he was in that gang we broke up. We only got back together when he promised he'd go straight. A week later he was arrested." She shook her head. "I should have listened to my dad and stayed far away from Donny. He was a real charmer but he never could stop lying and cheating."

Tom handed the copy to Vernon, who gave it to Vikki. "He's in 54C," said the latter.

"Are you sure?" asked Vernon.

"Absolutely. I never forget a room number."

CHAPTER 25

Vernon wasn't entirely sure about how to proceed. He'd dealt with irate customers before, and even violent ones. When they really turned nasty he usually called in Ravi and Beau, who were big, strong fellows and could handle any would-be brawlers and kick them out on their ear. Only once in his thirty-year career had he been forced to call in Chief Boelk and that was when he'd come face to face with a thief who'd broken into the office safe.

Now, though, he was going up against an actual member of the Bloods—or was it the Crips? A violent man with undoubtedly violent tendencies—maybe even in the possession of a firearm or other weapon he could turn on his assailants in a heartbeat.

"This is the time we call in SWAT," he told Tom as they gathered outside room 54C.

"SWAT won't come," said Tom. "It's up to us, Vernon."

"And us," said Vikki, who'd refused to stand down, insisting instead in taking down this dangerous-looking criminal who'd killed once and was probably ready to kill again.

"Maybe I should get Ralph," said Dee, who'd returned Jacob to the room and had returned with what looked like a snow shovel.

"Where did you get that?" asked Vernon, curious.

"It was in the shower."

Vernon gave Vikki a questioning look, but she gave him a look back that said, 'Don't ask me. I didn't put it there, boss.' Nor had she. Probably one of the guests had dragged it upstairs and the cleaner who'd done the room hadn't wanted to drag it downstairs again.

Dee was gripping that snow shovel like she meant business, Tom looked steeled and poised for action, and even Vikki had a vicious look on her face that indicated she was ready for action. Vernon could see there was no turning back from this: his associates were eager to get this Ernie Saddling or Marco or whatever the creep's name was dealt with immediately or even sooner.

So he took a deep and steadying breath, plastered his most severe expression on his face, and knocked on the door.

"Who is it?" a gruff voice sounded from the other side.

"I'm the hotel manager, Mr. Saddling. I was wondering if I could have a word?"

"I didn't order no room service!" the same gruff voice announced. "So go away!"

"This concerns a matter of some urgency, Mr. Saddling."

"I don't care. I'm resting."

"I'm afraid I have a key and I will enter if you don't open this door, Mr. Saddling."

"Oh, for Pete's sakes," muttered the voice, and there was some stumbling on the other side of the door, then it was suddenly swung wide and the same face that graced that fake driver's license suddenly stood before them, only it was actually towering over them, supported by a body that was easily twice as wide and a head taller than Vernon's. Up close and personal the thug's face was pockmarked and had a markedly unhealthy, pasty hue.

"Mr. Saddling?" Vernon asked, irresolution suddenly rendering him weak-kneed. "Mr. Ernie Saddling?"

"That's me. What do you want?" said the giant, his gaze raking over the small gathering standing on his doorstep.

"A matter of some importance has come to my attention," said Vernon, his voice more reedy than he would have liked. "It concerns the death of a guest, you see."

"So?"

"So as it turns out this guest was an associate of yours. A Mr. Donny Towns?"

The expression of hostility didn't waver, though the boxer's nose the man possessed slightly twitched, like Samantha Stephens, the lovable witch from *Bewitched*. Only this man didn't look lovable. Like Samantha, though, he could probably wipe them out with a flick of the wrist, and he didn't even need witchcraft to do it. "I don't know any Donny Towns."

"Donny Towns was in the same gang as you, Ernie—or should I call you Marco?"

"I don't know what you're talking about. My name is Ernie Saddling, and I'm a traveling salesman. I sell jewelry."

"Jewelry?" asked Vikki, piping up for the first time. "You mean like rings and stuff?"

The pockmarked face creased into a smile, displaying an actual gold tooth. "That's right. Rings and stuff. Are you in the market for a ring, darling?"

"Actually, I am. My boyfriend and I are getting married in the spring and we've been looking at some shops in town but so far haven't found what we're looking for, so—"

"Not now, Vikki," said Vernon.

"If the lady wants to buy a ring, the lady gets to buy a ring," said Ernie gruffly, and stepped aside to allow them in.

The small company filed into the room, with Ernie staring bemusedly at the snow shovel Dee had brought along. The giant ambled over to a small desk near the window, took a suitcase from underneath it and plunked it down on the bed, then snapped the latches and flicked it open. True enough, a nice assortment of rings and bracelets appeared.

"Ooh, can I have a look?" cried Vikki excitedly, completely forgetting about the mission.

"Of course you can, darling," said Ernie, aka Marco. "I've got plenty more."

And while Vikki inspected the collection of jewelry, the others just kinda stood there, looking around uncomfortably while Ernie gave his best impression of a tree.

"So about Donny Towns," said Vernon, finally finding speech again.

"Like I said, I don't know no Donny Towns," said Ernie.

"Oh, come on, Marco," said Professor Tom, clearly running out of patience. "His ex-wife recognized you. She said she saw you at Donny's trial. You and him were busted in the same sting operation and you served time at the same prison. And I'm sure that if we asked Wilfred Dobosh, the pensioner you tried to swindle out of his Mickey Mantle card he'd recognize you, too."

There were cracks in Ernie's armor, that much was certain. His stern expression was starting to waver, and he was now looking like a constipated tree, if trees got constipated.

"You cops?" he asked, gesturing at the Professor and Dee, the latter now gripping the snow shovel a little tighter.

"Professor Tom Kelly is a famous criminologist," said Vernon, glad of this opportunity to sing the Professor's praises again. "He's helped the FBI establish one of its most important departments, catching countless of the worst criminals in this country's history in the process." The

Professor winced, possibly out of admirable humility, but Vernon forged on. "Professor Tom is assisting me in nabbing Donny's killer and we have reason to believe we're this close to closing the case." He was holding index finger and thumb an inch apart, waving his hand in the giant's face, suddenly feeling triumphant.

But the giant wasn't going down without a fight. He grabbed Vernon's hand and squeezed it. Hard.

"Ouch!" Vernon cried.

"Look, I admit I was in on this baseball card scheme but I didn't kill Donny, okay? So whatever you think, Professor Whatsyourface, I didn't do it."

"Please release Mr. Haggis's hand," said Tom firmly.

And to Vernon's surprise—and relief—the giant promptly did.

"I think you did kill him," said Professor Tom now, pacing the room, his hands behind his back like the great detectives of old. "I think you decided you didn't want to split that million dollars and instead decided to keep it for yourself. So you killed your associate and flung him out the window, hoping his body wouldn't be found until you were far away from the scene of the crime, free to enjoy your ill-gotten spoils." He suddenly turned on Ernie. "Isn't that true, Marco?!"

"Oh, for Christ's sake, man, enough with the Hercule Poirot routine," said the hardened criminal as he threw a kindly eye at Vikki, who was now in the process of fitting rings. "Fine, I couldn't resist the temptation when Donny called and told me he had a sweet little deal lined up. A million bucks, ours for the taking, with no one getting hurt and no one about to go to the cops. The old guy would walk away happy with his fifty thousand smackers, and we'd be up half a million each, no harm done and only a day's work. But kill him? Nah. I'm not in that racket anymore. I'm a law-abiding citizen nowadays."

"Apart from the occasional rip-off," said Professor Tom.

The giant casually lifted his massive shoulders. "Like I said. It was a sweet deal. Donny was going to meet with the old guy, I'd check the merchandise, hand him this little suitcase full of gems—worth exactly fifty thousand. Deal was supposed to go through this morning, only Donny never showed. I figured he'd gotten cold feet and bailed on me."

"He did get cold feet," muttered Professor Tom thoughtfully. "Literally, in fact."

"So he's dead, huh? Murdered, you say?"

"Yes, he was stabbed," said Professor Tom.

"Too bad," said Ernie, clucking his tongue. He was taking the news rather well, Vernon thought. Then again, if he was Donny's killer he would, wouldn't he? "You know? In a way I'm glad. Cause for a moment there I thought Donny double-crossed me. Found himself another partner who could shift that baseball card. That's the only reason he got me involved. As a jewelry salesman I got contacts. Plenty of them. And Donny didn't. At least not the kind you need to set up a deal like this."

"You could have killed Donny when you figured you could pocket the full million," Professor Tom insisted.

"No, I could not. Like I said, I'm not a killer. And besides, Donny was holding all the cards, so to speak. He was the one who knew where to get the Mickey Mantle Topps Major League card. That was his side of the bargain. Without him, no card. Without me, no fifty thousand. That was the deal. So why would I kill him when I knew I'd end up with nothing if I did?" He was tapping his noggin. "That wouldn't be smart now would it, Professor?"

Vernon had to admit there was some logic in that. "Any idea who could have killed him?" he asked.

Ernie shook his head slowly. "Maybe he *was* trying to double-cross me. Got involved with another middleman who decided to go for the full payday instead of going halfsies? I don't know, buddy. I didn't know him all that well. We were business partners, not BFFs."

"What about his ex-wife Christy?" asked Tom.

The man mountain shifted his shoulders again. "No idea. All I know is what I read on *Page Six* and the kind of rags my wife picks up at the supermarket checkout. He was married then he got divorced and now he was getting married again to some superrich babe. Which just made me wonder why he needed to do this baseball card deal in the first place. He was going to marry into one of the richest families in the country, dude. So why the hustle?"

CHAPTER 26

Why the hustle indeed? Tom asked himself as he and Dee returned to their room. Ernie—also known as Marco—had shaken his confidence that they'd found the killer and now he didn't know anymore.

"Do you think he did it?" he asked his wife.

"He struck me as an earnest man," said Dee. "At least for a crook."

"So you don't think he's our guy?"

"Honestly? At this point I have no idea. Though he made a great point. Only a week from now Donny was going to be rich beyond his wildest dreams. So why did he try to hustle poor Mr. Dobosh out of all that money? That just doesn't make sense."

"No, it doesn't. Unless he was such a player he couldn't pass a great hustle when the opportunity presented itself."

"And risk everything? Risk going back to jail and lose Tracy Hall?"

Dee was right. Why would Donny risk everything just so he could make half a million dollars? Or was it something about the psychology of the man? Perhaps it didn't feel right that he came into this marriage empty-handed? Maybe he wanted to offer Tracy an expensive gift? To show her he wasn't just some bum she was marrying?

Or could it be that the money was to set up his ex-wife Christy and their baby?

They'd arrived back at their room and Dee shoved their keycard in the door and it clicked open. Scott was on the bed playing a computer game on his phone and Maya was flicking through a copy of *Cosmo* she must have found downstairs. Neither teenager looked up. The only one who did was Ralph, who greeted them with a happy woof and came bounding over to press his nose in Tom's hands. He grinned down at the dog. At least one member of this family was happy to see them.

"Did I tell you about Maya meeting Tracy?" asked Dee. "Or me meeting the great Mr. Hall himself?"

"No, you did not," said Tom, taking a seat on the foot of the bed.

"And tell him about me and Ralph finding that knife, Mom," said Scott without looking up from his phone. "Oh, that's right. You already know about that." He then did look up. "You have to give me that knife back, Dad. Me and Ralph want to have another crack at it. I'm pretty sure that with one sniff Ralphie will rout out that nasty killer for us."

In a few words, Dee apprised her husband of all that had happened that afternoon.

"My, my, you guys have been busy," he said at story's end, then added his own story to the others, and it was a testament to the power of Mr. Dobosh's tale that even Scott forgot all about his computer game for a moment and awarded his dad his full attention.

"So this Marco character didn't do it?" asked Maya.

"Honestly? I don't think he did," said Tom. "Though these are inveterate liars, so who knows?"

"What about Christy?" asked Maya. "Tracy seemed pretty convinced she did it."

"I don't know, honey," said Dee. "My crime-dar is pretty wonky these days."

Maya laughed. "Your crime-dar has always been pretty wonky, Mom. Remember how you couldn't believe that your assistant had stolen that painting from your gallery last year? Only when the cops showed you CCTV footage of her cutting it out of its frame and tucking it into her bag did you finally figure out she was the one who'd tried to rip you off."

Dee grimaced at the memory. It had not been her finest hour. Tom patted her hand. "If it's any consolation I thought she was the best assistant you ever had, too, honey."

"Me, too," said Dee. "I even considered her a friend."

That 'friend' was now languishing in prison, and Dee had become a lot more discerning about who she let into her life. So did Tom, after a few similar past mishaps had turned ugly. Unwilling to dwell on that now, he returned his attention to the case at hand. Then Scott's words came back to him. It was a long shot, true, but wasn't it worth trying? And when Ralph gave a soft bark, he smiled. So it was decided then, to give this crazy scheme a spin.

CHAPTER 27

"Come on, boy," said Scott excitedly. "Show us what you got. Let's go!"

Ralph, his tail wagging, looked from the knife he'd been sniffing to Scott, the dog's intelligent eyes gleaming. The rest of the family all stood in Vernon's office, witnessing this unique experiment. Mom, cradling Jacob, skeptical but willing to give it a try. Maya, even more skeptical, and Dad, who, surprisingly enough, had agreed to go along with the gag.

And then there was Vernon, of course, the manager who'd needed quite a lot of convincing to open his safe and hand them the knife. Then again, judging from the dog portraits in the guy's office it was obvious he was a big dog person, and a dog person simply couldn't look at Ralph and not fall in love with the lovable mutt!

Vikki, meanwhile, was the final person present, and she seemed happy enough. She was real pretty, too, Scott thought, with her blond hair and her big smile. Pity she had a boyfriend, or else he would have loved to ask her out. Not that his folks would have let him. They figured that at twelve he was way too young to ask girls out on dates. Lame-ohs.

And so it was that Scott was grinning at Vikki, who was returning his smile and making him feel all giddy inside. But then suddenly Ralph gave a loud woof and he was off!

"The game is afoot!" Dad cried, whatever that meant.

Scott held Ralph on a loose leash, even though he would have preferred to let go of the leash altogether. But there were a lot of people around now, with dinner coming up soon, and Mom and Dad didn't want to risk Ralph scaring the crap out of some doddering old folks who might get a scare when they saw this big dog bounding up at them at full tilt.

Not that Scott could imagine anyone being scared of Ralph, who was the sweetest, kindest, loveliest dog alive!

He had a hard time keeping up as Ralph galloped through the lobby and straight into the dining room, slaloming between people already gearing up for dinner and engaging in some preprandial conversation, if preprandial was the word Scott was looking for, and then he shot through those swinging doors and into the kitchen!

Ralph, followed by a fired-up Scott, followed by Mom and Dad and Maya and Vernon with Vikki bringing up the rear, all filed into that kitchen and then the weirdest thing happened: Ralph, without hesitation, launched himself at a round-faced young woman dressed in a cook's uniform, put his paws on her belly and barked up a storm, happy to have reached destination's end.

"Eeeeek!" the woman yelled.

"Woof woof woof!" Ralph barked.

"Good boy!" Scott cried.

"Down, boy, down!" Dad screamed.

"What's this horrible dog doing in my kitchen?!" a tall blond man shrieked.

"She did it!" Scott said, pointing at the woman. "She's the killer, Dad!"

Ralph, who was like a dog with a bone, wasn't about to let all this shouting deter him from finishing his mission. So he barked some more, jumped up against the woman some more, and finally gave her face a good old big lick with his long tongue. She screamed, and then did something Scott had never seen anyone do in real life before: she actually fainted!

Or at least she sank to the floor, her eyes fluttering, and started breathing heavily.

"What have you done!" the tall blond man with the cook's costume shouted. "You killed my cook! You people have just killed my cook!"

"Calm down, Sam," said Vernon. "Alfa isn't dead. She's just overwrought. Isn't that right, Alfa?"

The woman muttered something incomprehensible and Mom yelled, "Bring her some water. A glass of water! Quick!"

"Who are you to give me orders in my own kitchen?!" the man called Sam screamed.

"Water, Sam, quick," said Vernon, and grudgingly the blond man did what he was told, filling a glass of water from the tap and carrying it over to this Alfa person.

Meanwhile, Scott had dragged Ralph away from his hapless victim, and was taking him outside where it was cold and wet and dark and still windy and terrible. At least there Ralph could get all this barking out of his system, Scott thought. And he was right. Within a few minutes the dog was howling plaintively, scratching at the kitchen door to be allowed back inside.

When he opened the door, the heat of the kitchen blasted Scott's face. Alfa was seated on a chair, a glass of water in her hand, and she was looking dazed but alive.

"Take Ralph back upstairs," Dad ordered the moment he caught sight of them.

"But, Dad! He caught the killer! He should get a reward!"

"Now, Scott!"

Grumbling, Scott did as he was told, and took Ralph out of the kitchen, through the dining room and up the stairs. Nice. Being punished for being the hero of the hour.

"It's all right, Ralphie," he said, patting the dog's head. "You saved the day."

CHAPTER 28

In the kitchen, Dee was holding the cook's hand. She was still a little pale around the nostrils but was gradually becoming herself again.

"Why did that dog attack me?" she asked plaintively. "I don't understand."

"It's fine, Alfa," said Vernon. "Everything is fine."

"He just came up to me and attacked me. You saw that, right?"

"He didn't attack you," said Dee. "He was playing a game, and he thought you were the target. Ralph would never attack anyone. He's very playful and very sweet."

Alfa's eyes widened. "He's your dog? You sicced your dog on me?"

"Professor Tom did not sic his dog on you," said Vernon, stressing the 'professor' part. "Professor Tom would never do that. All he did was conduct a little experiment."

"Oh," said Alfa, and nodded. "Okay. I'm sorry. I'm not very good with dogs. They never seem to like me very much. And I'm afraid the feeling's mutual most of the time. Except when they're small. My sister has a Chihuahua and she's fine with me and I'm fine with her. But your dog..." She glanced at Dee. "Your dog is big. I thought he was going to bite me."

"Ralph would never bite you," Dee assured the cook. "He just wanted to play with you."

Alfa grimaced, her round face remorseful. "He picked a bad partner to play with, didn't he? What kind of experiment were you running, Professor Tom?"

"We'll explain later," said Tom.

By now the kitchen was full of people, and they were all listening, eager to know what was going on. This hadn't escaped Sam Kwiek's attention, and the chef now clapped his hands. "Back to work, you lazy lot! Dinner will be served, whether you like it or not. Chop, chop and on the double and all that!"

When everyone had returned to work, Dee and Vikki escorted Alfa out of the kitchen and into the dining room, where they sat her down in a quiet corner. Tom and Vernon and Maya joined them.

"I should be in there," said Alfa, pointing at the kitchen. "Sam will be furious. He doesn't have a lot of people to help him, you know. It's just me and a couple of others."

"You can go back if you feel you're up to it," said Vernon, "and not a moment sooner. Sam will just have to improvise. Now there are a few things I would like to ask you, Alfa."

The woman nodded, her cheeks quivering as she did. "Ask away, boss."

Vernon held up the Ziploc bag with the knife. "Have you ever seen this knife before?"

She studied the knife for a moment, then understanding seemed to be dawning and she pressed a fist to her mouth, biting down on her knuckles. "Is that what I think it is?"

"If I think what you think is what I think, you're thinking right," said Vernon gravely.

Alfa held out a quaking hand in the direction of the knife,

as if on the verge of grabbing it, then reeled in the hand again. "This is the knife that killed Hot Gangster, isn't it?"

"It is," Dee confirmed. "And what we'd like to know is whether you've seen it before."

"Or handled it, even," said Vikki, eagerly following the conversation.

"'Oh. My. God! That's why that dog attacked me! He thinks I did this! He thinks I killed Hot Gangster!" She turned to Vernon and grabbed his lapels. "I didn't! I didn't kill him! I would never do this! I would never kill anyone! You have got to believe me, boss!"

"I do believe you, Alfa," said Vernon kindly. "For one thing, you had absolutely no reason to kill Mr. Hot Gangster. You didn't even know him, did you?"

"Only from what I read about him on Facebook. He was hot, wasn't he? I mean, I know a lot of girls thought he was smug, and of course he was a gangster and gangsters are bad news, but he was hot. I liked his eyes. He had beautiful eyes. I always said with eyes like that he couldn't have been all bad. I mean you can tell a lot about a person just from looking into his eyes, and when I looked into his eyes—on Facebook, I mean, not in real life. I never met him in real life, even though I would have liked to—before he died, I mean. Now that he's dead I don't want to meet him—so when I looked into his eyes I saw he was a kind soul. And a soul like that would never do anything to hurt another human soul—or even another human being if you see what I mean." She frowned. "What was the question again?"

"Did you ever handle this knife?" Vernon asked, jiggling the little baggie.

She stared at the knife as if mesmerized. "That knife ended the life of a good man. That knife is evil." Then she seemed to snap out of it. "I would never handle that knife if my life depended on it, boss. That knife is the personal property of Chef Kwiek and he's made it perfectly clear that anyone who touches that knife will be gutted and scaled."

"Did he now?" asked Vernon, intrigued as he studied the knife.

"So you never touched this knife?" asked Dee, just wanting to get this clear.

Alfa looked sheepish. "Oh, I've touched it. It's only the finest knife in the kitchen. Very sharp. Gets the job done. Perfect for peeling an apple. Or an orange, for that matter."

"So you've touched it," said Tom, settling back.

"Only me and everyone else. When Chef Kwiek isn't looking, of course. He's nasty."

"Yes, he is," said Vernon, deflating a little.

"Can I get back to work now, boss?" She gestured at the dining room quickly filling up. "Otherwise there's gonna be a lot of people angry about dinner being late."

Vernon nodded. "If you feel up to it, please do, Alfa. And we're sorry about the dog."

"Never mind about the dog," said Alfa, getting up. "It just gave me a big old fright is all." She locked eyes on the knife for a moment. "Can't you, I don't know, check that thing for fingerprints and DNA and whatnot?"

"As soon as the storm blows over and the police get here that's exactly what we'll do," said Vernon, sounding tired. "But for now we're left to our own devices, I'm afraid."

Alfa seemed to chew on those words for a moment, then its full import suddenly came home to her and she threw her hands to her face. "Oh. My. God! The killer is in here with us, isn't he! He's right here in this here motel with us!"

"Yes, he is," Vernon confirmed. "So if you have any information you would like to share with us, Alfa—or if you can think of anything that might shed light on what happened to Mr. Hot Gangster, please let us know."

She nodded ten times in quick succession, stalked off

towards the kitchen, then returned, still nodding. "If I know something, I'll tell you, boss. Only I don't know nothing."

And then she was off for real, and Vernon sighed deeply. "I don't know nothing. If that doesn't apply to all of us I don't know what does."

"At least now we know that Alfa handled that knife," said Maya.

"And so did everyone else in that kitchen," Vernon pointed out.

"So why did Ralph single her out?" asked Dee.

They all chewed on that for a moment, until Tom voiced the thought they all shared: "I have absolutely no idea."

CHAPTER 29

To say that he was upset was the understatement of the century. Samuel Kwiek, known to his friends, of whom he had very few, as Sam, was feverishly washing his hands. Dinner was over and a minor miracle, too, as far as he was concerned. He didn't have his usual staff at his disposal, instead having to put up with rank amateurs like Beau Snoop and Alfa Robston, who didn't merely look and behave like a pair of clueless waiters but who actually were a pair of clueless waiters.

Alfa, after having thrown a hissy fit because some fluffy little pooch put his paws on her, had returned to her station to wreak more havoc, and Beau had very nearly destroyed the pumpkin soup by stirring in too many bell peppers.

At least dessert had been easy: blueberry shortcake sundaes, straight out of the freezer. Speaking of the freezer, he suddenly had a thought. All through dinner prep he'd been ruminating about the loss of his very best carving knife. He missed that knife. It was almost as if he couldn't function properly without it. Like missing a limb. And now he couldn't help but wonder: where was it? Sam had briefly checked the body before and hadn't seen the knife but that didn't mean a thing, did it? It was Beau who'd told him the knife should have been lodged into the dead man's chest but what if he was wrong?

Beau Snoop was a fool and a moron. Could it be he'd simply looked in the wrong place? Could it be, therefore, that his knife—the knife he'd got as a prize after winning the cooking competition Kitchen Heroes at the tender age of fifteen in his hometown of Vught in Holland—was still lodged firmly inside that loser Hot Gangster in some other spot?

He methodically dried his hands and glanced around. The kitchen was emptying out, the only people still present the dishwashers plunging pots into the deep sinks on the other side of the kitchen and operating the industrial-sized commercial dishwashing machine.

Unseen by anyone, therefore, he yanked back the handle of the walk-in freezer and stepped inside. He immediately set foot for the dead gangster. Yanking back the tarp, his sharp eyes raked the man's frozen body, which now resembled a life-sized popsicle, until he discovered the red spot on the man's blue pajamas. Darn it. Snoop was right after all.

Sam's lips formed a thin line when he realized his precious knife was gone. Gone!

And fat chance getting it back from the police once they took charge of this preposterous investigation and retrieved it. And he was just about to draw the tarp back over the man when he spotted something. Something shiny located in the man's hand.

He bent over and narrowed his eyes. It wasn't a knife but it was something. His curiosity piqued, he tried to remove it from the frozen gangster's fingers. It was hard going, as they were closed around the tiny object. Luckily it was small and finally emerged from between the frozen digits. Sam held it in his own hands and studied it for a moment. It was some kind of brooch, he now saw, shaped like a butterfly. Gold and inset with tiny stones that could very well have been diamonds. The eye of the butterfly was a nice little ruby.

Classy. At least for a lowly gangster.

But then the door to the freezer opened and Beau walked in.

"Will you need me for anything else, Sam?" asked the waiter.

"No, that'll be all," he said, drawing the tarp back over the dead man.

"Sad business, isn't it?" Beau remarked.

"There's a saying in my country, Beau," said Sam. *"Boontje komt om zijn loontje."*

"Sounds… ominous."

"Freely translated it means 'What goes around comes around.' I guess this man got what was coming to him." And with these harsh words, he walked out after Beau and closed the door to the freezer behind them.

Five minutes later he was entering his room, thinking about this and that, when he suddenly noticed he was holding a tiny little thingamajig in his hand. He stared at the thing, then remembered what it was and grimaced. Vowing to hand it over to Vernon in the morning, he tucked it away in his desk drawer, lay down on the bed, and flicked on the TV.

An episode of *Kitchen Nightmares* had just started and he settled in for the duration.

CHAPTER 30

Tom got up. Like Vernon, he was feeling slightly dejected. This thing seemed like one of those giant jigsaw puzzles: the ones you want to lay your hands on as a kid only to discover they're a lot harder to figure out than you anticipated. He was a pretty smart guy, but this murder had him stumped. He then remembered something and turned to Vikki.

"Christy Cadanet claims she left the hotel this morning to go for a walk. By any chance do you remember seeing her leave?"

But Vikki was already shaking her head before he finished the question. "I wasn't here this morning, remember, Professor? I only arrived when Daisy's shift was over. Just in time for the storm," she added. "Just my luck, I guess. I should have been the one who took the night shift, but Daisy needed the day off so we switched at the last minute. And now I'm stuck here with this murder business while she's off at home watching the Kardashians."

Tom wasn't sure how the Kardashians featured into this story but by now he figured everyone and anyone featured into the story so why not simply go with it? So he nodded. "Thanks, Vikki. The phone lines still work, right? I mean the landline?"

"Sure."

"Could you perhaps call Daisy on the phone and ask her about Christy?"

Vikki displayed her pleasant smile. "Of course, Professor. I'll do it right after dinner."

"I appreciate it." He saw that Maya and Scott had already taken their seats at their usual table, and that Scott had had the good sense to leave Ralph upstairs in their room.

"Let's have dinner," Dee suggested. "I'm starving."

Jacob produced a soft gurgling sound and in spite of himself Tom had to laugh. "I guess the little guy is hungry, too, huh?"

"We're all hungry, Tom. So let's forget about this murder business for a moment and just have dinner as a family."

"Extended family," he said as he watched Jim and Eden take their seats, too.

"I like that couple," said Dee as they walked over. "They're nice."

"Yeah, I like them, too. Plus, it's always handy to have a doctor in the house."

"Two doctors, no less."

They joined the rest of the company and as Tom glanced around, he saw Christy Cadanet arrive for dinner, her baby on her arm, and take a seat on the other side of the dining room. The Halls were also there, father and daughter, and he noticed how Tracy Hall studiously ignored Christy, even as Christy intently studied the woman who'd stolen her husband. There was obviously no love lost between those two. Good thing there was a wide swath of other tables and guests between them.

Ernie 'Marco' Saddling also walked in—and wouldn't you

know it? He took a seat at the same table as Wilfred Dobosh. Tom wondered what they would talk about, since Ernie didn't know Mr. Dobosh was the guy he'd tried to swindle, and Mr. Dobosh didn't know he was sharing dinner with his swindler's associate and would-be fence.

Christy knew, though, for Tom watched as she stared daggers at Marco.

"Where are you, honey?" suddenly asked Dee. "You seem miles away."

She'd placed her hand on the back of his head and was lacing her fingers through his hair. He smiled and looked down at his plate. "It's all these people. Marco and Mr. Dobosh and Christy and Tracy. All brought here because of Donny Towns. And even now, when he's dead, they're still locked in here, at daggers drawn, even if some of them don't even know it. It's just that... that man, resting in that freezer, created a lot of trouble for a lot of people."

"You're still on that investigation then, are you?" asked Jim.

"Yeah, I still haven't found what I'm looking for," Tom confirmed.

"Dad, that song is ancient," said Scott, rolling his eyes.

Alfa and Beau were doing double duty tonight, as they'd both been enlisted to help dole out dinner, and even Vernon was sticking around, overseeing the proceedings. And as Tom tasted his pumpkin soup, he thought it tasted a little funny. Then again, it just might be his mood that affected his taste buds.

"Maybe you need to step back and try and look at the big picture," said Eden.

"What do you mean?" asked Tom.

"Well, you've been puzzling together all these clues and stuff, right?"

"Uh-huh."

"So maybe now it's time you put it all together, if you see what I mean."

"Have a family meeting!" Scott cried, excited. Then his face sagged. "We don't have a whiteboard, though."

"Who needs a whiteboard?" asked Maya.

"That's how the cops do it," said her brother. "They put all the pictures of all the suspects on a big whiteboard and then they connect them with squiggly lines and stuff. I've seen it on *Castle*."

"You watch *Castle*?" asked his sister dubiously.

"Hey, that Beckett is hot!"

"You don't need a whiteboard, son," said Jim, tapping his temple. "All you need is this."

Scott frowned at him. "Your finger?"

"Look where my finger's pointing!"

"Your… liver spot?"

"My head! All you need is that noggin of yours to figure this out. And you've got four noggins between the four of you."

"Five, if you count Jacob," said Dee, feeding the baby a piece of broccoli. He didn't seem to like it for immediately he spat it out again. The broccoli described a perfect arc through the air and landed on Eden's plate. Dee, mortified, said, "I'm so sorry, Eden!"

But Eden was laughing. "That's all right, Dee. I've handled my share of babies."

"You have babies?" asked Scott, wrinkling his nose. "But you're so old!"

"Scott!" Dee snapped.

"He's right," said Eden. "I am pretty old. But once upon a time I was young, Scottie. And I raised five boys just like you—hell-raisers, every single one of them."

"You raised five boys?" asked Dee. "I admire you, Eden. I really do."

"I admire her," said Jim, with a crusty smile. "I still don't know how she did it."

"How we did it," said Eden, leaning into her husband and patting his arm. "It wasn't always easy, but we managed pretty well, didn't we?"

"They're fine boys," Jim confirmed. "All grown up now, of course, with families of their own. In fact that's the reason we came down to Ohio in the first place. Our eldest lives near here. We were just coming back from visiting him and his newborn when we got stuck in that blasted storm. Good thing we found this motel." He smiled at them. "And some very nice people to be riding out this storm with, too."

"That's very kind of you to say, Jim," said Tom. "We're glad we met you guys, too."

"Even if we're a couple of ancients," said Eden, with a wink at Scott, who shrugged.

CHAPTER 31

After dinner, Dee felt like going straight to bed. It had been a long day, and she was bushed. Jim and Eden also didn't feel like sticking around, and together the two families walked out of the dining room and into the lobby. They paused for a moment in front of the door, gazing out at the world outside, and marveling at the storm that seemed to have reached a fever pitch by then.

"Amazing, isn't it?" asked Eden. "How a storm like that unleashes these amazing powers? Nature truly is a force to be reckoned with."

"As long as it doesn't blow away this motel I'm glad," said her husband.

"Do you think it will get that bad?" asked Maya, concern lacing her voice.

"Well, they did say winds will pick up to about forty miles per hour."

"Is that bad?" asked Scott.

"Yup. That's pretty bad, Scott. Especially with this kind of whiteout. You see, the wind will blow the snow around so that after a while you can't see a thing in front of your eyes."

"Better to be nice and warm inside," said Dee, hugging Baby Jacob close.

"So does that mean I can't take Ralph out tonight?" asked Scott.

"Well, it is pretty cold out there—even for Ralph," said Jim kindly.

"But what if needs to go?"

"I think a short potty break will be fine," said Tom. "In and out, like before."

"You got to be careful that his paws don't freeze, though," said Jim.

"You seem to know a lot about dogs," said Tom.

"Oh, we had plenty of dogs in our time," said Eden. "Kids and dogs, right?"

Dee smiled. "Maybe you need to bundle Ralph up, Scott."

"Bundle him up? You mean, like, dress him up in a sweater or something?"

"Or you could outfit him with little socks to protect his paws," said Jim.

They all laughed at that, but Dee thought it was not such a bad idea. If Scott was going to take Ralph out in these conditions maybe it was best to dress him up a little. He was a furry dog but even fur wouldn't be unaffected by these extreme conditions.

They'd moved to the staircase and were mounting them to the second floor. Soon they arrived at their destination and both families said goodbye, Jim and Eden disappearing into their room while the Kellys walked a few doors on to theirs.

And as they settled in for the evening, Dee was happy that for once conversation hadn't been dominated by the murder case. It was nice to be a regular family again.

Scott had thought about this. In fact he'd thought so hard he'd even neglected his smartphone for once, which just lay there on the nightstand, forlorn and forgotten, its shiny lights blinking each time a message arrived or someone liked something Scott had posted on Snap or Insta or Facebook or even when some app decided to send him another notification.

This idea Jim had put into his head needed seeing through: he didn't want poor Ralph to freeze to death when he went for his evening poo and wee.

So first he decided to confiscate some of Jacob's socks—he had plenty to go around, after all—and slipped them on Ralph's paws. Ralph wasn't too happy about this sartorial experiment. In fact he tried to remove the pink woolly socks with his teeth. Not that he managed, but he whined about it so much Scott decided to remove them again until it was Go Time.

And then there was the issue of keeping Ralph's body temperature up. One of Dad's sweaters would do just fine. As it happened Mom had packed Dad one of his ugly Christmas sweaters—the red one with the reindeer—just because she thought Dad liked them so much and they made him look like a handsome young Santa—Mom's words, not Scott's. But Scott knew for a fact that his dad hated those sweaters. He'd heard him say so himself on the phone when he was talking to Grandpa. They'd even laughed about it.

So Scott was actually doing his dad a favor when he snuck the sweater out of Dad's suitcase while he and Mom were in the bathroom brushing their teeth.

All that was left was something to put on Ralphie's head, and Scott had just the thing. Grandma had knitted Jacob a little cap when he was born and if he stretched it out a little it was a perfect fit for the big fluffy dog.

So Scott tucked all these supplies into a plastic bag, shoved it under the bed, and then bided his time until Ralph decided he needed his bathroom break.

A recap of *The Voice* was playing on TV, so he and Maya watched it for a while, then Mom and Dad, too, when they were done in the bathroom, Mom and Maya on one bed and Scott and his dad on the other. The contestants were all pretty much crap today, none of them singing very well, and the worse they sang the more effusive the coaches sang their praises and urged 'America' to vote for them. As if anyone was fooled by that lame tactic.

Soon enough the entire family was zonked out, and someone must have turned off the TV at some point for silence reigned in the room, only interrupted by the even breathing of four Kellys and one dog and the occasional snorts of Kelly Number Five—Dad.

Scott was awakened when something was scratching at his arm, which was dangling to the floor.

When he opened his eyes, he found himself looking into the trusty eyes of Ralphie.

"What's wrong, boy?" he murmured, rubbing his eyes.

Ralph tilted his head, and gave a soft whimper.

Oh, dang it. He'd totally forgotten to take the dog out!

Excitement shooting through him, he slipped from the bed, careful not to wake Dad, who was lying on his back, his mouth open and producing soft snoring sounds. On the other bed, Maya and Mom were both fast asleep, Maya still clutching her phone as if it was a lifeline to a better and saner world and Mom's hand on Baby Jacob's leg, as if to make sure he wasn't going anywhere. And as Scott dragged the bag with Ralph's winter supplies from under the bed, Jacob made smacking sounds with his lips, Mom muttered something, Maya clutched her phone tighter to her chest, and Dad produced an extra-loud snort.

Scott paused for a moment, but no one woke up, so he slipped his feet into his shoes, shrugged into his thick coat, grabbed Ralph's goodie bag, and tiptoed to the door, Ralph right by his side, tongue lolling and tail wagging.

Finally. It was Go Time!

CHAPTER 32

"Come on, boy," said Scott once he'd closed the door behind him, but Ralph didn't need any encouragement, already tripping deftly ahead, happy to be out and about again.

The lights were on in the corridor, but then they probably always were, and Scott pulled on his knitted cap with the fleece lining and checked the contents of the bag.

Yep. Ralph was going to be so happy!

They descended the stairs to the lobby, where the Christmas tree was merrily blinking away in a corner, then through the dining room once more and into the kitchen.

Ralph knew the way by now, for he trotted on ahead, then came bounding back, giving soft woofles, as if to say: 'What are you waiting for, you slowpoke?!'

"Easy, boy," said Scott, laughing, when Ralph gave him a shove in the backside.

Inside the dining room the lights were doused and Scott figured it was best to keep them that way. So he fired up the flashlight app on his phone and wended his way through the tables. He knew the routine by now, and so did Ralph. Finally they reached the kitchen door that led outside, and Scott crouched down, placed his phone on the tile floor and took out his Dad's Christmas sweater, Jacob's socks and Jacob's cap, then began to outfit Ralph with this assortment of winter clothes. The socks and the cap were a good fit, but the sweater was too big for the dog. So Scott simply tied the arms around Ralph's belly and finished it off with a nice knot.

"There," he murmured as he admired his handiwork. "That should do the trick."

Ralph was staring up at him with a sad look on his furry face, then produced a soft whimper.

"Now don't you complain," said Scott. "This is to keep you from freezing to death."

And then he flung the door wide and the dog forgot all about his predicament and bounded outside, straight into those forty-mile-an-hour winds.

Well, maybe Jim had exaggerated, for the wind wasn't blowing all that hard. Still, it was pretty chilly out, and there was so much snow in the air that it was hard to see a thing, even with the flashlight app. The light didn't penetrate beyond a few feet. Ralph, who'd gone bounding off, soon returned, and when he did, it was minus Jacob's socks, minus Jacob's knitted cap, and minus Dad's ugly Christmas sweater!

Oh, boy. If Mom found out Scott had lost that sweater there would be hell to pay!

So Scott ventured out into that terrible whiteout, keeping his head down and shielding his eyes against the wind and the sleet that seemed to slice right through him.

"Where did you lose it, buddy?" he asked when Ralph joined him. "Show me."

But Ralph had no intention of showing him anything. He probably was glad to be rid of those garments and didn't want them found. Maybe he'd even buried them where they would never be found.

Scott soon gave up the search. He'd simply come back in the morning, when it was light out, and look for that sweater again. It wasn't as if Dad would miss it overnight. In fact he never wore it, only when Mom insisted he did.

And as Scott returned to the kitchen door, he was glad to be back inside. Ralph wasn't all that pleased, and it took a bit of cajoling on Scott's part to get the dog to toe the line and join him in the kitchen.

All this being outside in that icy cold had made Scott a little peckish, so he directed his phone around the kitchen, hoping the chef had left a nice apple pie out or something. Or even a cheese sub. Or a fruit bowl. No such luck, though. And he balked at checking the freezer. No way was he going in there in the middle of the night when that dead gangster was laid up. For all he knew he was a zombie and came alive at the stroke of midnight!

And that's when he saw it: the door to the freezer was ajar!

His eyes snapped to that lock, and instantly he knew: someone was in there.

"Quiet, boy," he whispered to Ralph.

His heart beating a steady drum, Ralph panting next to him, the dog's coat wet and dotted with tiny bits of snow and ice, Scott switched off his flashlight app, crouched down next to one of the ovens and waited.

Light flashed inside the freezer—whoever was in there had a flashlight thingy just like he had. This was just eerie. Could it be that one of the motel guests had gotten a hankering for a little midnight snack? Or that Chef Kwiek was working on his next-day menus?

Or it could be that someone was taking a peek at Hot Gangster's dead body!

Scott watched intently for what felt like the longest time, his eyes adjusting to the darkness. Then finally there was movement. That flashlight was dancing across the kitchen floor now, and the door to the freezer was closed with a thumping sound. He couldn't see who the other person was, though, and Ralph was getting antsy, producing a soft whimper.

The figure halted in its tracks, and then they were shining that flashlight all over the kitchen, the beam bouncing across gleaming steel surfaces and appliances and tabletops.

Scott held his breath, not wanting to be caught by this freaky nocturnal prowler.

Not that he didn't have every right to be here, but a thought had just occurred to him: what if this was the killer, who'd returned to take another look at their handiwork!

After a moment, the prowler seemed satisfied that they were alone and moved through the kitchen and then through the swinging doors and into the dining room.

Scott made to follow, Ralph right on his heel, and glimpsed through the porthole. The prowler had reached the end of the dining room so Scott eased open the door and moved through, along with Ralph, then eased the door back, not wanting it to start swinging. He tiptoed through the dining room, carefully maneuvering along the tables, which were set for breakfast, the light from the lobby guiding his way, and then he was taking a quick peek around the corner, hoping to finally catch a glimpse of this mysterious snoop.

He extended his head like a shy chicken would, and was disappointed when all he saw were two black-clad legs moving up the stairs. Dang it.

"Come on, boy," he told Ralph. "Let's see who this creepy crawler is."

As one, boy and dog moved up the stairs, careful not to be seen or heard, and when they arrived on the landing, Scott looked first in one direction, then the other, and was gratified when he saw the person he was stalking move along the corridor, now in full view.

Whoever it was, they were dressed for the occasion: black leggings, black sneakers, black sweater, black cap. Almost like a cat burglar. Definitely not someone out for a midnight snack. And definitely not Sam Kwiek, who seemed to live in his chef's uniform.

And as Scott stared daggers at the prowler's back, hoping to catch a glimpse of his or her face, suddenly the sneaky cat burglar opened a door to the right and disappeared inside.

Darn it!

Scott quickly made his way over, and was surprised to find that the room the night prowler had disappeared into was… 24B!

CHAPTER 33

*D*ee was the first one to wake up. She usually was. The moment first light slanted through the curtains, she was up and about. She padded over to the window and peered out. Nothing. Complete whiteout, just like the day before. She sighed. How much longer were they going to have to stay here like this?

She glanced at her husband and son, sharing a bed and sleeping the sleep of the dead. Scott was lying spread-eagle, his limbs indiscriminately thrown in every direction, while Tom was on his back, his arms folded across his chest. He looked like he was ready for his own funeral. Maya was face down as usual, a little string of drool tracing from the corner of her lips to the pillow. The dog, meanwhile, was at Scott's feet, mimicking his master.

Why was it, Dee thought, that even though they'd gotten the dog as a family, Ralph was most attached to Scott? Maybe because he played with him the most? And gave him the most attention? But it was Dee who fed him and took him to the vet and washed him and gave him his flea tablets.

She shook her head, then moved over to Jacob and

rubbed the baby's belly. Jacob opened his eyes and grinned happily, crowing and wiggling his arms and legs with glee.

He was such a happy baby, and such a quiet one, too. Unlike Scott and Maya, who'd been criers, both of them.

Dee yawned, and thought today might be a great day for Tom to wear his nice new Christmas sweater his mother had made for him. It might cheer them all up. Infuse the day with some of that festive spirit.

She dragged the suitcase from under the bed and started rummaging through its contents. She hadn't had the energy to unpack yesterday, so they were effectively living out of their suitcases. When she didn't find the sweater, she frowned. She was pretty sure she'd packed it. Huh. Weird.

When she got up, she saw that Scott was rubbing his eyes and stretching. "You'll never believe who I saw last night," he said by way of a morning greeting.

"Last night? Where were you last night?"

"After you guys fell asleep I took Ralph for a walk." He swung his feet from the bed. "Someone was in the kitchen freezer, so I followed her up the stairs until I could see who it was."

"Her?"

He nodded, then yawned cavernously. "Christy Cadanet. Dressed in black, like a cat burglar."

Dee thought about that for a moment. "What was Christy doing in the freezer in the middle of the night?"

"Beats me. Maybe she was saying goodbye to her husband?"

"Maybe. But why sneak around like that? She could have just asked Vernon."

Ralph, who was wide awake by now, had jumped from the bed and was scratching the door, whining up a storm.

"Make him shut up!" Maya was groaning, burying her head deeper into her pillow. "I want to sleep!"

"Time to wake up, sleepyhead," said Dee. "It's almost eight. Time for breakfast."

Tom was also stirring, but still holding steady in his death pose.

Scott had also noticed the strange phenomenon. "Why does Dad look like Dracula sleeping in his coffin? Does he always sleep like that?"

"As a matter of fact he does. Though to be fair, Dracula sleeps in the daytime."

Scott had moved to the window and before Dee could stop him, had opened it.

"Huh," said Scott. "Looks like that blizzard finally gave up."

"Impossible," said Dee, and joined her son. But he was right. It was still snowing, but not as hard as the day before. The wind had died down, too, and the world was silent and white but a lot less hostile and scary. She checked the window. It was completely caked with ice, top to bottom, which is why at first glance it looked as if the blizzard was still raging.

Scott was getting dressed. "Guess I'll take Ralph for a walk again," he muttered.

"Maya can do it," said Dee. And when Maya loudly protested, she added, "Scott has been walking him all day yesterday. Fair is fair."

"Oh, God. I feel like I haven't slept a wink," Maya muttered.

"You slept like a log," said Scott. "I watched you sleep. With that death grip on your phone. Probably kissing that screensaver with that picture of your boyfriend all night."

"I was not kissing my phone all night! And what were you doing watching me like some kind of pervert, you pervert?!"

"What can I say? I'm a nocturnal creature," said Scott with

a shrug. "I probably got that from Dad, who it turns out is Count Dracula. Who knew?"

Just then, there was a knock at the door. Scott, who was closest, opened it, and immediately Ralph ran out, bumped into Vernon, who was the early visitor, and both man and dog went down in a heap of tangled limbs.

Tom woke up with a snort, rocketed up in bed and yelled, "Hoedown!"

"Oh, boy," said Scott. "A vampire hoedown at dawn. What a family."

※

After extricating himself from Ralph, with the help of Scott, Dee and Maya, Vernon patted the few remaining hairs on his head back into place and got up.

"Sorry to disturb you this early," he said. "But is the Professor up?"

"Dad just got up," said Maya.

"He was fast asleep," said Scott. "Even vampires like Dad need their beauty sleep."

The reference was clearly lost on the motel manager, who appeared anxious.

"I'm up," said Tom, smoothing down his blue twill pajamas with the pink stripe. He looked like a college professor even when he just got out of bed, Maya thought.

"There's been a development, Professor Tom," said Vernon anxiously. He was glancing left and right down the corridor. "May I come in and apprise you all?"

"You may," said Maya, amused by the man's politeness. No wonder he and Dad got on so well. They both shared that same academic stiffness.

Vernon entered and quickly closed the door behind him.

"Alfa came to me this morning," he said the moment he

was in. "She remembered something last night. Something very important. A clue!" he added, waving a scholarly finger. "Isn't that right, Professor? How a good detective loves a good clue?"

"Yes, he certainly does," said Dad. "So what was this clue?"

Vernon swallowed. "It's that knife again, Professor. Frankly I couldn't sleep all night. Kept on thinking about this dreadful murder business. You probably couldn't sleep either."

"Sure," said Dad after a moment's hesitation, and Maya smiled behind her hand. In spite of the thrilling events of the previous day, the entire Kelly family had slept like a rose.

"So Alfa kept thinking about that knife—why would the dog finger her? And then she got it—Christy Cadanet ordered room service yesterday morning. And do you know what she ordered?"

"I have absolutely no idea," said Tom.

"A cheese platter!"

It was pretty clear to Maya that this should have meant something to them, judging from the feverish look on the manager's face. Dad blinked a few times, then said, "A cheese platter?"

"A cheese platter!"

"Interesting," said Dad.

"Right? And since it was Alfa's turn to handle room service, she was the one who brought up that platter. And because she likes that one knife so much—the one Sam Kwiek made such a hoopla about—she decided to add it to the platter. For cutting," he explained when everyone stared at him as if he'd said something silly. Even Ralph seemed confused.

"Oh!" said Dad, understanding finally dawning. "So Alfa handled that knife—the knife went up to Christy's room with the cheese platter, and was used to murder Donny!"

"Exactly! So you see, Christy is the one we want. She ordered that platter!"

"Or maybe Donny did," said Dee, pointing out a flaw in Vernon's reasoning.

"Yes, conceivably so," the manager conceded. "I'd have to ask Daisy if she remembers who ordered that platter. At any rate, it doesn't matter. Now we know that knife was in the room—and Christy must have used it!"

"Unless someone else came in and used the knife on Donny," said Dad, whose mental faculties were finally making a comeback. Maya knew her dad was never at his best before he'd had his first coffee so this was a breakthrough. "I asked Vikki to ask Daisy if she remembers Christy going for that walk she mentioned. Has she mentioned anything to you?"

"No, she has not," said Vernon decidedly, as if Vikki had personally insulted him. "I will ask her right away." He then gestured to Dad's funky pajamas. "Will you and your family be joining us for breakfast?"

"We will," Dee assured the manager. "As soon as we're ready we'll be down." And as the manager turned to leave, she added, "And Scott has something to tell you, too. Isn't that right, Scottie?"

"Christy snuck into the freezer last night," Maya's brother said. "Dressed like a cat burglar."

"Christy Cadanet?" asked Vernon. "Sneaking into the freezer?"

"Yup. Middle of the night. I was walking the dog."

Vernon stared at him as if he'd grown a second nose, then cut his eyes to Dad. "Looks like the plot is thickening, Professor Tom."

"Like molasses," Dad agreed, which Maya thought was something only a college professor could say with a straight face.

CHAPTER 34

"So what have we got?" asked Dee as she combed her hair. "Christy ordering a cheese platter with the murder weapon—or it could have been Donny who ordered it. At any rate, that would explain how the knife got into that room. Then we have Tracy Hall and her dad who were supposed to meet Donny, presumably because he wanted to introduce them to his ex-wife and his baby and hopefully instigate some kind of reconciliation."

"Then we've got Marco meeting Donny Towns so they could rip off Mr. Dobosh," Tom went on. "Though he claims he never saw Donny and thought he'd stood him up."

Scott had already gone downstairs to see if breakfast was being served, and Maya had reluctantly agreed to take Ralph for a walk but not before dressing up as if she was about to brave a snowstorm—which she was.

"So the way I see it," said Dee, "is that this Marco character could be lying and that he did meet Donny and the two of them had a fight and Marco fatally stabbed Hot Gangster and chucked him out the window while Christy was out for that walk. Or… that Christy, for any number of reasons, got mad at her ex-husband and killed him in a fit of rage."

"Possible motives being that she was still upset that Donny left her for another woman and things came to a head when she saw him again. Or that she discovered he wasn't there to meet her but to hustle Mr. Dobosh out of his baseball card. Or even that he suggested she meet Tracy so they could all hug it out and forgive and forget and—"

"Instead she stabbed him and killed him." Dee shrugged. "Makes sense to me."

"So our prime suspect is Christy Cadanet?"

"If I were a cop I'd say she fits the bill," said Dee.

She liked Christy, and when she spoke with her had felt for the woman. But the evidence was piling up, and she could have been lying all this time.

"I wonder why she snuck into that freezer last night. It couldn't be to find that knife. She knew Vernon had put it in his safe. So why?"

"Beats me," said Dee. "Guilt? Heartache? One last kiss?"

"Eww," said Tom, putting on his shoes. "Kissing a dead person?"

"He's not just a dead person to her, Tom. He's the man she loved all her life."

And that was the tragedy of this case, Dee thought. Christy had loved Donny and he'd betrayed her over and over again. How much can one woman take before she snaps? Even if Christy had killed her ex-husband, a jury would probably take these extenuating circumstances into account. See things from her point of view. Dee knew that she did.

She then frowned, remembering something. "Have you seen your Christmas sweater, Tom?"

*S*am frowned before him, glowering at no one in particular. It was his standard facial expression. He'd read somewhere that after the age of forty a person's face more or less gets stuck in its default expression. If you tend to scowl a lot, that's the way you'll look when you hit the big four-oh. And if you're a peppy person, the same logic applies: hence the reason some people look cheery all the time, while others look like they swallowed a bug.

Sam didn't care. In fact he thought his face helped him in his work. A chef needed to inspire obedience and respect in his kitchen team. A smiley face doesn't get the job done.

He opened his drawer to take out his watch and discovered the tiny object he'd taken off Hot Gangster last night. His scowl deepened when he remembered the dead dodo. If word ever got out that a dead person had been inside that freezer all this time Sam's name would be mud. He'd forever be associated with the gruesome Grand Guignol scene.

Then again, it wasn't as if his career was hitting highlight after highlight. More like rock bottom after even rockier bottom. Being chef at the Gateway Lodge wasn't exactly the same as being chef at Le Bernardin in New York City or the Robuchon au Dôme in Macau.

So how had he got here? Being fired from his last position as a sous-chef in Chicago's Alinea restaurant after he'd cursed out an arrogant customer hadn't helped. Or before that, slapping a cook across the face in New York's Eleven Madison Park when the fool dared suggest a slight alteration to Sam's recipe. Things had quickly gone downhill from there and now here he was, at the bottom of the heap, a 'chef' at a roadside motel of all places.

Still, he had his pride, and if the price to pay for that pride was a career detour, so be it. Motel or no motel, he was still a chef, and he had menus to create and people to feed.

So he got up from the bed, snatched the trinket from the drawer, and walked out.

Downstairs, he saw Vernon, who was in the middle of a heated conversation with Vikki, who was holding the phone. He walked up to the manager and handed him the gem.

"What's this?" Vernon demanded, casting a furious look at the little bijou.

"I have absolutely no idea," Sam said, not enjoying being spoken to in this manner, nor being given the evil eye the way Vernon was now doing. "But it's all yours, Haggis."

"I don't want it and I don't need it!" Vernon sad hotly, and handed the thing back.

"I picked it up in the freezer," Sam explained haughtily. "I think you should have it."

"Probably belongs to some woman," said Vernon, and returned his attention to Vikki, a clear sign that the conversation was at an end and he considered the matter dealt with.

"Fine!" Sam huffed, and strode off.

He walked into the kitchen, his personal domain, and saw a young woman or girl stomping her feet in the kitchen door, an icy gust of wind wafting through the usually overheated space. He frowned, wondering what she was doing in his kitchen, and why the door was open. Then he had a bright idea. He swiftly joined her and held out the brooch.

"Hey. You," he snapped.

The young woman turned at the sound of his voice, then her eyes dropped to the piece of jewelry.

"You're a woman, aren't you?" he asked a little brusquely.

She frowned. "How did you guess?"

"Here," he said, pressing the thing into her gloved hand.

"What's this?" she asked, studying the gold bauble.

"I'm not an expert but I would say it is some species of brooch."

She looked up, confused. "Why are you giving this to me?"

"Why not?"

"Where did you find it?"

"In the freezer. I took it off that corpse." Then, feeling he'd spent as much time and attention on the silly little gem as he was prepared to, he nodded curtly and stalked off. Now it was someone else's problem, and he could finally return to what he did best: cursing out his underlings and creating Middletown's best meals for the lowest possible price.

CHAPTER 35

Maya stared at the brooch. It was a nice brooch, as brooches went: it was shaped like a butterfly and dotted with tiny diamonds with a cute little ruby forming the butterfly's eye. She turned it over in her hand until she saw the inscription. *'D-To loves Pookie.'* Cute.

She tucked the little trinket into the pocket of her coat and promptly forgot about it.

Ralph, who was still giddy with excitement, was hopping around the snowdrifts like a young pup. To Maya's relief, the snowstorm seemed to have lost a great deal of its power overnight. It was still huffing away but it was clear its heart wasn't in it anymore. And a good thing, too. If she had to be cooped up in this motel for two more days she'd go bananas.

She glanced ahead of her and all she saw was snow.

She glanced to the left and the same thing: the world was white.

Then she turned to the right and saw an eyesore: an overturned black garbage bag.

For Christ's sakes. Couldn't the kitchen staff take out the

trash? Didn't they realize garbage attracts rats and mice and other vermin? At least if they survived this arctic blast.

A sheet of paper had dropped from the garbage bag and gotten stuck between the wall and the bag. Maya pried it loose with a groan of frustration. God, she hated littering.

She cast an idle eye at the piece of paper. Bored out of her mind now, and freezing, she blinked when she saw that it was a bill for services rendered. And when she saw the name of the client and read the neatly typed up message from the purveyor of this particular service, her eyes went wide and her jaw went slack.

Holy cow. This changed everything, didn't it?

"So now we know," said Vernon as he accosted Tom in the lobby.

"Know what?" asked Tom.

"Know who ordered that cheese platter!"

"Oh, right," said Tom. "And? Who ordered the cheese platter?"

"It was definitely Donny Towns," said Vernon, licking his lips. "Daisy remembers very distinctly, even though the name he gave her was Adam Plauder, of course."

"Of course," said Tom. Dee had gone on into the dining room with Jacob, and now Scott was bounding down the stairs, his limbs more or less rolling along, looking like a latex version of himself, and gave his father and the manager a one-fingered salute in passing.

"So you see what this means, right? It means the knife was there in the room!"

"What about Christy?" asked Tom. "Did Daisy see her go out yesterday morning?"

"No, she did not!" cried the manager triumphantly. "She most certainly did not!"

Tom rubbed his chin thoughtfully. This wasn't rocket science. It was obvious to him that Christy Cadanet was the killer. So now what? They couldn't arrest her. They couldn't lock her up either. All they could do was wait for the police to show up.

"Have you called this Chief..."

"Boelk. No. I thought I'd wait to hear what you said. You're the expert, Professor Tom. You're the one with all the experience. I defer to your judgment. You know that."

Tom winced slightly. Sooner or later he'd have to come clean. Maybe better later. "I think you should call Chief Boelk and explain to him what we know. He'll have to decide."

Vernon smartly tapped him on the shoulder. "I'll do just that right this instance!"

And off he went to his office to get the Middletown chief of police on the phone.

Just then, Christy Cadanet came down the stairs, her baby in her arms. She gave Tom a slight nod, then walked right past him. Tom had the strange sensation that she knew they were onto her. But what could she do? Where could she go? The hotel was on lockdown.

He followed her into the dining room, his eyes burning holes in the woman's back. A murderer. An actual murderer. It was a novel experience for sure.

Once more, he took a seat at the same table with Jim and Eden. The couple looked fresh-faced and rosy, a good night's sleep having done miracles for their constitution.

"And? Have you cracked the case, Professor Kelly?" asked Jim with a grin.

"I might have," he confirmed. "Now it's up to the police to make an arrest."

Dee had finished placing Jacob in the high chair the motel provided. "Are you sure now?" she asked. "Did Vernon get the confirmation he needed?"

"Yes, he did," Tom said, and watched as Christy sat down for breakfast not three tables away from them. "In fact he's on the horn with the chief of police right now."

"This is all very exciting, isn't it?" asked Eden, who was buttering a piece of toast.

Breakfast was set out on a buffet table, but Tom wasn't feeling particularly hungry. The toast or the scrambled eggs or the fried sausages didn't appeal to him, nor did the orange juice or the different kinds of breakfast cereal, all set up in large containers. The only thing he wanted—the only thing he needed—was a cup of hot, strong black coffee.

And he'd just gotten up to get himself that cup when Christy suddenly accosted Tracy Hall, who'd entered the dining room with her father. Christy was screaming something at Tracy, and when Tom hurried over to prevent another murder from being perpetrated, he heard her scream, "You did this! You killed him!"

CHAPTER 36

It wasn't hard for Maya to figure this out. She might not be an ace detective or even an amateur one but this was as simple as A-B-C. So when she arrived in the dining room, a happy Ralph on the leash, and saw Christy Cadanet tear into Tracy, she wasn't surprised.

Her dad, who'd positioned himself between the two screaming women, seemed a bad fit as a referee. His face was red and he'd planted his hands on his hips, staring down at the floor. Meanwhile Tracy was screaming, "Do you even listen to yourself? You're crazy, lady! You killed him and you know it. In fact we all know it—isn't that right, Professor?"

Dad, dragging his eyes up from the floor, seemed reluctant to enter into the fray, even though at some point it must have seemed like a good idea. "It's not my position to…" he began, then segued into, "The police need to look into…" and finally concluded, "Perhaps we better take this…"

"Outside!" Christy yelled. "You damn right we better take this outside." She was eyeing Tracy viciously. "You and me— we settle this right now—what do you say?!"

"I'm not going anywhere with you," said Tracy. She was pointing a very pointy nail at the other woman. "You're going to jail—and your baby is going to social services."

That was the wrong thing to say, for Christy now launched herself at her nemesis, claws out, and Tracy screamed as she tried to get away. No such luck, though, for Christy's aim was true as she took hold of a nice chunk of blond hair and dunked Tracy to the floor.

But now everyone was in the dining room, and strong hands quickly dragged a kicking and screaming Christy from the billionaire's daughter and restrained her.

Vernon came hurrying up. "They're coming!" he was saying. "Chief Boelk will be here in less than an hour. The storm has blown itself out and the weather is improving fast."

"Well, that's good news at least," said Dad. Mom had also joined them, and Scott, and they were all staring at Christy, the most likely suspect.

"Maybe we should lock her up," Jim suggested, gesturing to Christy. "She's the guilty one, isn't she?"

Vernon nodded. "Looks like. Chief Boelk agrees. And so does Professor Tom, and he's the expert."

Jim quirked an eyebrow at Dad, who had the decency to blush.

"Before you lead her away," said Maya, stepping forward, "there's something you all need to know."

She felt a little dizzy, speaking up in front of all of these people, but she knew she had to, before a gross injustice was done.

"What's wrong, honey?" asked Mom.

"I need to say this, Mom," said Maya, and took the brooch from her pocket.

All attention snapped to the trinket. "Chef Kwiek gave

this to me just now. He said he found it on Donny's body." She turned to the chef, who was scowling as usual. "Where did you find this, exactly, chef?"

"Does it matter?" he gruffly asked.

"Yes, it does. It matters a great deal."

"In the dead man's right hand."

"You took this out of the dead man's hand?" Vernon cried. "Are you crazy?"

"I offered it to you but you told me to give it to a woman," Kwiek snapped. "So I did."

"He gave it to me," said Maya. "There's an inscription on the back." She turned the brooch. "'*D-To loves Pookie.*' It didn't ring a bell at first, not until I remembered something I read on *TMZ* not so long ago." She smiled at her brother. "You were right, Scott. I love that site." She took out her phone. "It's an article about Donny and his new girlfriend Tracy Hall. Some pap got a shot of Donny leaving a tattoo parlor in Manhattan. And a closeup of the tattoo in question, located on his hand, right between his thumb and his index finger. It's a little heart with the words, 'D-To loves Pookie,' D-To being Donny Towns and Pookie being…" She turned to Tracy, who was staring daggers at her. "Tracy Hall."

All eyes turned to Tracy, who stood tapping an annoyed foot, her arms folded across her chest. "So what? Donny had a brooch in his hand he was going to give to me. A present."

"I think he gave you that brooch a long time ago," said Maya, now feeling like a regular Miss Marple giving her final little speech. "And you wore it proudly. The only reason it would be in his hand would be if he grabbed it off you as he was falling from the window after you stabbed him to death."

Gasps of shock now rang out all around her, but Maya was going well and not about to stop. Tracy was still looking smug, though. "You're talking out of your tush, sister. We all know Christy killed Donny. She couldn't stand it that he left her for me." She spread her arms. "I mean—why would I kill my fiancé? I loved him. We were getting married next week."

"I think Donny was having second thoughts," said Maya.

"Oh, please," said Tracy. "That man adored me. Everybody knows that."

"You said you and your father were invited here by Donny so you could meet Christy and her baby and settle this feud, right? Even though you weren't too happy about it?"

"That's right. Donny wanted to do the right thing by Christy and the baby. He was an honorable man."

Maya produced the piece of paper she found. "This says otherwise."

Tracy stared at the document, the color draining from her face. "What's that?"

"This is a printout of an email from a man named Rider Mainwood. It was sent to you the day before yesterday. Marked extremely urgent and for your eyes only."

Maya watched as Wilbur Hall looked up, startled. It was obvious Tracy had never shared this particular email with her father.

"Mr. Mainwood runs a private investigation business out of Arkansas," Maya went on. "The cleaner must have thrown the printout in the trash—or maybe you did, Tracy—and it ended up in the motel garbage, where I just found it." She glanced around at her attentive audience, even Scott momentarily stunned into silence. "I'm guessing this is the email you showed to Donny, as proof of his infidelity. Let me read to you what Mr. Mainwood wrote. 'Suspect in Gateway Lodge Motel meeting ex-wife and kid. Happy reunion. Sharing a room. Photographic proof of infidelity available. Link provided. Password Cheater69.'" She looked up, Tracy's face a mask of anger. "I checked the 'photographic proof of infidelity' and those pictures are pretty steamy, Tracy. Steamy enough to make you fly out here immediately to confront your fiancé."

Tracy was exchanging furious glances with her father.

"You better shut up, Trace," her father said. "Not another word, you hear?"

"So what happened, Tracy?" asked Maya. "Did you wait for Christy to leave the room and then you went in to confront Donny and things got out of hand? The knife was nearby, probably lying on the table next to the cheese platter Donny had ordered. So you grabbed it and stabbed him, didn't you? And then he stumbled out of the open window—only he snatched that brooch from your blouse just before he did. And you couldn't very well go down there and get it back, could you? So you snuck downstairs last night and into the freezer to get your brooch back—yes, my little brother saw you."

"But... I saw Christy," said Scott, confused.

"You saw *someone* go into their room—which you thought was room 24B. But in actual fact you saw Tracy go into her room, which is located right next to Christy's."

Tracy's eyes snapped to Scott. "You jerk!" she screamed, and launched herself at him. Only before she ever got close, Ralph gave a sharp bark and jumped up at the berserk young heiress, knocking her off her stride and to the floor, then stood barking over her.

"Get this monster off of me!" Tracy hollered.

Dad took Ralph's leash and dragged him off a cowering Tracy, who got up with the help of Mom. "I'm sorry, dear," said Mom. "He doesn't bite, you know. But he doesn't like it when you attack the members of his family."

Tracy stood there for a moment, tears now rolling down

her cheeks. She glanced over to her dad, who was shaking his head. "Oh, Pookie," he said softly, looking crushed.

"I'm sorry, Daddy," she said. "It was an accident, you know. Donny was a big, nasty brute and he slapped me. He-he even tried to strangle me. I had to defend myself, so…"

That didn't sound very plausible, Maya thought, but decided to leave well enough alone. The police could take things from here. And as the thought entered her mind, there was a commotion at the entrance to the dining room, and three police officers came hurrying in, led by a burly man with a walrus mustache and jowly cheeks.

"Chief Boelk," said Vernon, relief clear in his voice. "Finally. It's her. She did it."

The chief nodded, his hand going to his belt where a pair of shiny handcuffs were dangling. "I know." He then strode up to Tracy. "Christy Cadanet?"

"Christy didn't do it, Chief," said Vernon. "Tracy did. Tracy Hall."

The Chief glanced around for another young woman, then his eyes settled on Christy. He purposely walked up to her. "Tracy Hall, you're under arrest for—"

"I'm not Tracy, though," said Christy. "She's Tracy."

The Chief now scratched his mustache. "I'm confused," he confessed.

"It's been a very confusing two days, Chief," said Dad. "Tracy Hall just confessed. She killed Donny because he was cheating on her with his ex-wife Christy Cadanet. That's Tracy over there and this is Christy."

"Right," said the Chief gruffly. "And you're the brilliant criminologist Thomas Kelly, founder of the FBI's Behavioral Science Unit? The man who wrote the book on profiling?"

"Um…"

The Chief grimaced. "I didn't think so. So why don't we

let these nice folks finish their breakfast, and you and me and these two ladies go into Vernon's office and thresh this thing out once and for all?"

"Sounds like a good idea," said Dad, speaking as though he had a frog in his throat.

CHAPTER 37

The Highlander's engine was ticking over nicely—thanks to the good people of Triple-A who were working overtime these days—and the Kellys were ready to start the final leg of their trip. Jacob was settled into his baby carrier, crowing happily and trying to catch a fat fly who had miraculously survived the snowstorm, and Tom, Dee, Scott and Maya were saying goodbye to their host and to Jim and Eden, the old couple who'd become friends over the course of the past two days.

"I don't know how to thank you, Professor," said Vernon, clasping Tom's hands affectionately.

Even though Chief Boelk had revealed Tom's secret, Vernon was still a believer.

"And I don't know how to thank you, Vernon," said Tom. "You've been the perfect host."

"Oh, one does what one can," said Vernon modestly.

"No, you've got a great little motel here, Vernon," said Jim. "And I for one am prepared to give you a star rating on TripAdvisor. Isn't that right, darling?"

"I'm surprised you even know about TripAdvisor," said his wife.

"My son taught me all about the Interwebs," Jim fondly told Dee.

Dee smiled. She was glad this trip was over, but Tom was right. It had been quite the experience, and not all of it as bad as one would imagine, giving the circumstances.

The storm had finally blown over—a lot sooner than the weather forecasters had predicted, but then weather forecasters usually got it wrong—and it was time to head back to Seattle and pick up the thread of their lives. Scott and Maya and Tom might just make it back in time for school, and Dee had a gallery to run.

Vikki, who'd also come out, stood wiping away a tear. "You guys are the most wonderful guests," she was saying. "Please come back next year."

"We might," said Dee. "Usually Tom's folks visit us in Seattle for Thanksgiving, but this was a nice change of pace."

But Maya was throwing her pleading glances, and so was Scott. They clearly weren't as keen to come back to Middletown, Ohio—or Dayton—as she and Tom were.

"At least you solved the murder," said Eden. "Or at least your brilliant daughter did." She pinched Maya's cheek, who smiled a little polite smile.

"Just putting two and two together," said Maya modestly. "Once I saw that brooch and remembered that *TMZ* story, and then of course the email, things clicked into place."

"They should make *TMZ* a subject in school," said Scott. "The things you can learn from reading that site are unbelievable!"

Maya pinched him on the arm, and this was not a loving pinch either.

"Ouch!" Scott cried, and tried to pinch his sister right

back, but she slapped his hand away. A slapfest followed, and Dee cried, "Cut it out, you guys!"

"Listen to your mother," Tom grumbled when the slapping intensified.

"Oh, just let them be kids together," said Eden with a maternal smile. "They have their whole lives to behave and be good. You'll be surprised how quickly the years pass." She heaved a little sob, and pressed her hand to her face.

Jim massaged his wife's back. "Five boys. And gone in the blink of an eye," he said kindly. "Appreciate what you got, folks, that's all I can say."

They watched Maya chase her brother around the car, slipping and sliding, then start a snowball fight, and Dee shook her head. Maybe Jim and Eden were right. Then again, if Maya killed Scott or the other way around, she'd kill them both. Though she had to admit Maya had surprised her with the clever way she'd solved this murder. And she'd stunned Chief Boelk, too. When the Chief had finally slapped the handcuffs on Tracy, and arrested her for the murder of her fiancé, he'd told Maya it was all thanks to her, and had suggested a career in law enforcement might not be such a bad thing for her to consider.

As for Tom, the Chief had told him in no uncertain terms that a career in law enforcement was the last thing *he* should consider. Apparently the Chief was a big fan of the TV show *Mindhunter*, and had even read the book the show was based on. And unlike Vernon he could count and had immediately deduced there was no way Tom had been old enough to found that particular institution in the year of our Lord 1972.

"Do you think Tracy Hall will get the punishment she deserves?" asked Vernon.

"I doubt it," said Tom. "She'll insist she acted out of self-defense, and given Donny's reputation the jury will probably accept it. Plus, she'll have the best lawyers money can buy."

"At least everyone will know what she did," said Vikki, hugging herself against the cold. "And that's a punishment all in itself, isn't it?"

They all chewed on that for a moment, but then it was time to head on out. And just when Dee had managed to corral both Scott and Maya into the car, after saying goodbye to Jim and Eden and Vernon and Vikki, she noticed they were missing one family member.

"Where's Ralph?" she asked, searching around.

"Probably looking for another dead body," said Vernon in a dubious display of black humor.

"Ralph!" Dee yelled, putting her hands to her mouth. "Ralphie!"

And there he came, bounding up to them from around the back of the motel.

"He's got something between his teeth!" said Jim excitedly. "Looks like you were right, Vern. He found himself another stiff!"

Ralph came running up, and Dee saw they were right: he was carrying something between his teeth. She crouched down. "What you got there, boy? Give it to me."

Ralph obediently dropped the object at her feet, then gave a cheerful bark, as if to say, 'I found this especially for you!'

Dee picked it up and studied it. It was a piece of cloth, ripped from something.

"What is it?" asked Vernon.

"Looks like one of them Christmas sweaters," said Jim.

"Them horrible ugly ones," Vikki added. "With the reindeer."

"Oh, God," said Vernon. "When I said that about another dead body I was only kidding!"

And then Dee recognized the swath of sweater. It was red

and had a piece of antler on it. Her eyes snapped to Scott, who was looking at her with a sheepish and obviously guilty expression on his face.

"How was I supposed to know he was gonna lose the darn thing!" Scott cried. "I just wanted to make sure he didn't freeze to death, just like Jim told me!"

"Oh, so now it's my fault, is it?" said Jim.

In spite of herself, Dee had to laugh, and then Jim and Eden did, too, and Vernon and Vikki. Even Tom was laughing, probably because he realized he'd never have to wear that sweater ever again, and Scott, because he was getting off pretty easy.

The only one who wasn't laughing was Maya. Instead, she stuck her head out of the car. "Can we get going already? We're gonna miss our flight, you guys!"

And then they were finally off, five Kellys and their dog. They'd found a dead body, solved a murder, survived a blizzard, and had made new friends in the unlikeliest of places.

Time to head on home—where new adventures and mysteries awaited.

EXCERPT FROM MURDER RETREAT (NORA STEEL BOOK 1)

Chapter One

Bobbi tapped her pencil against the yellow pad, frowning darkly at no one in particular. When the tapping didn't produce the desired result, and neither did the frowning, she finally threw down both pencil and pad with a groan of frustration and swiftly rose from the couch she'd been lounging on.

"I can't do this," she muttered, and stalked over to the kitchen.

"Can't do what?" asked Melody, her blond head popping out from the landing.

"Plot this sucker," Bobbi said as she yanked open the fridge and checked around for something edible. She was a voluminous woman and it took a lot of food to keep that body in the shape it was accustomed to. She saw a tub of Trader Joe's Belgian Chocolate Pudding and grabbed it. She grunted in approval. Just what she needed right now.

Without further ado, she yanked away the cover, grabbed

a spoon from the dish rack, plunged it into the chocolaty gooey goodness and stuffed it into her mouth.

Closing her eyes, she savored the delicacy.

"Leave some for the rest of us, will ya?" a voice sounded nearby.

Opening her eyes, she saw that Zita was staring at her.

"I wish you wouldn't do that," she grumbled as she dug in for another spoonful.

"Do what?" asked Zita.

"Sneak up on me like that."

"I didn't sneak up on you."

"Yes, you did. You sneak up on people and you scare the living bejeesus out of them."

Zita rolled her eyes. "Whatever."

Melody, who'd come bounding down the stairs, joined them in the small kitchen. "So what's the trouble?" she asked.

"Trouble with what?" asked Zita, now intently studying her fingernails, which were painted a glossy black, her favorite color. She was a wiry young woman with raven hair and a distinctive lip piercing, currently wearing a Lisbeth Salander T-shirt and ragged black jeans.

"Bobbi's having trouble plotting out our next book," said Melody.

"Oops," said Zita.

Oops was right. In this collaboration of theirs, they'd agreed from the first that everything began with plot. Bobbi provided the plot for the books, Melody sprinkled in the romantic sizzle, and Zita added her own brand of dark suspense. But without a plot to start off with they were sunk. It was the foundation upon which the rest had to be carefully built.

"Maybe we can think up a plot together?" Melody suggested.

Zita scoffed, "Yeah, right."

A peppy, happy blonde, Melody's forte was romantic banter, not plotting. She was, after all, the romance author of the trio, her own novels as successful as Bobbi's thrillers and Zita's horror output.

Three authors working in three different genres, they'd met at a writer's conference five years ago and had hit it off immediately. They couldn't be more different and yet there had been an instant rapport. Hanging out after late-night karaoke the third night of the conference, they'd decided to work together, and create a joint pen name they could all contribute to. Nora Steel had been born that night, and the first novel saw the light of day soon after. A series of romantic suspense novels featuring feisty heroine Janet Lee Parker was the result, the sales of Nora Steel novels quickly surpassing their individual output.

"But if you can't think up a plot we're sunk," said Melody now, her cornflower blue eyes wide. "Sunk!"

"Oh, I'll think of something," said Bobbi, ladling more pudding into her mouth. "Have I ever let you down before?"

"Well, there was that one time when Janet Lee broke up with Jack Black," Zita reminded her.

"They got back together in the next novel. No harm done."

"Readers hated us for that," said Melody, smiling at the memory. "Hated us."

"Readers don't like cliffhangers," said Bobbi. "But sales of the next book went through the roof."

"Maybe you can kill off Jack?" Zita suggested.

Melody turned to her, her cupid's-bow mouth forming a perfect O. "You can't!"

"Why not? Talk about a cliffhanger. And the next book you simply bring him back."

"Back from the dead," Bobbi muttered, nodding. "I like it."

"Kill Jack? You wouldn't!" Melody cried.

"Or we could kill off Snookie," Zita continued.

"No!" Melody cried. "Not Snookie!"

Snookie was Janet Lee and Jack's teacup Maltese. They'd adopted him in book three and had never looked back. Now Snookie was a fan favorite. She even had her own fan club.

Bobbi grimaced. "If we kill Snookie there will be hell to pay."

Zita grinned. "At least they won't be able to accuse us of being predictable."

"No," said Melody. "I'm putting my foot down on this one. Snookie lives, and so does Jack."

Zita sighed. That's what you got from collaborating with a romance novelist, that sigh seemed to indicate. Always going for that happy end. In her own novels Zita liked to explore dark themes and all manner of murder and mayhem, but they'd made a pact when they first created Nora Steel: every decision had to be agreed upon by the three of them.

"Oh, all right," said Zita. "But I think you're being silly. A romantic suspense novel should have suspense, and what better way to create suspense than killing off a fan favorite?"

"No means no," said Melody, her face a mask of determination. "As long as I have a breath in my body, Snookie will never die, and nor will Jack or Janet Lee."

"Spoilsport," Zita muttered.

Just then, a fist pounded the door of the cabin they were staying at, and the three friends looked up in surprise.

"Are we expecting someone?" asked Zita.

"Nope," said Bobbi.

"Lois?" Melody suggested.

Lois was the housekeeper who kept the fridge and the larder stocked and made sure the cabin was looking spic and span at all times.

"She never comes in before lunch," said Bobbi, frowning.

She dumped the empty tub of Trader Joe's Pudding in the trashcan and moved towards the door.

The log cabin where they were currently holed up, hard at work on the next Nora Steel novel, was located in Upswing, Georgia. Dotted with similar cabins, the North Georgian forested setting provided the requisite peace and quiet writers needed to produce their next masterpieces.

Bobbi paused in front of the door for a moment, then threw it wide. When she found herself face to face with none other than Martin SS George, the famous fantasy writer, she blinked in surprise. The bearded scribe gave her a wide grin and held up a meaty paw.

"Howdy, neighbor."

Chapter Two

MSSG, as the fabled and much-lauded writer was affectionately called by his fans, was a bearlike presence with a Santa Claus twinkle in his eyes and signature black fisherman's cap firmly lodged on his head. Tiny white curls peeped from beneath the cap, adding to the Santa Claus look. He pushed his wire-rim glasses up a bulbous nose and beamed at them.

Melody thought he looked exactly like the pictures she'd seen. A sweet grandpa.

"Mr. George," said Zita, practically genuflecting before their famous colleague.

"Just call me Marty," said the writer with a chuckle.

"I love your work," Zita gushed. "Especially *Game of Bones*, of course."

"Thanks. And I have to say I'm a big fan of your Janet Lee Parker books."

"You know Janet Lee?" asked Melody.

"Of course I know Janet Lee. Who doesn't? Your books

have taken the writing world by storm. Three consecutive New York Times number one bestsellers? I've read them all and I love them. Especially Snookie. I'm a big fan of Snookie."

"We were actually thinking about killing off Snookie," said Zita, earning her a prod in the ribs from Melody.

Marty's smile vanished. "Kill off Snookie? Why would you kill off Snookie?"

"Well, you kill off popular characters all the time," said Zita with a shrug.

"That doesn't mean you should," said the writer, who looked visibly upset. "How can you kill off a cute, sweet, innocent little doggie like Snookie? That's just plain cruel!"

"We won't kill off Snookie," said Melody. "Zita was just kidding, weren't you, Z?"

"Actually—ouch!" Another prod in the ribs and Zita gave Melody her best glare.

"So what brings you here, Mr. George?" asked Bobbi.

"Marty, please." He arranged his bearded visage into an expression of apology. "The thing is—I'm guessing you're here for the same reason I am. To write a book, right?"

"That's right. We're hard at work on the next Janet Lee Parker," Bobbi confirmed.

"And I'm slaving away at my next doorstopper," said Marty, nodding. He threw a quick look over his shoulder, then lowered his voice. "See, the thing is, I got this housekeeper who keeps my fridge stocked and my cupboards overflowing. Only, somehow my wife has managed to convince her I've given up smoking but I haven't." He took off his cap, fiddled with it and gave his best impression of Puss in Boots, directing an imploring look at the three of them. "Do you happen to have a cigarette? Any brand will do. I'm not fussy."

"I'm sorry, Marty," said Melody. "But we don't smoke. Do we, girls?"

As there was no reply, she turned to look at her two co-writers. Bobbi looked sheepish. "I only smoke when I finish a book," she said. "I keep a celebratory cigar just for that occasion."

"You smoke?" asked Melody, aghast.

"Like I said—only when I finish a book."

"You wrote a dozen books last year."

"So I smoked a dozen cigars last year."

Melody turned to Zita, who was giving her a cool look. "Yeah, I smoke. So what?"

"Could you…" Marty began, and both Bobbi and Zita nodded and moved off.

Marty gave Melody a slightly embarrassed look. "You're a lifesaver, Miss Steel."

"My name actually isn't Steel," said Melody. "It's Pen. Melody Pen. Nora Steel is the name we use when we write together."

"Of course, of course. And a fine name it is." He glanced beyond her at the cabin's interior. "I see yours is slightly bigger than mine. Have you been coming here long?"

"This is our third year, actually. Do you come out here a lot?"

"Oh, yes. I do all of my writing out here. I love it. Absolutely love it. Couldn't write anywhere else."

He'd stepped inside and stood looking at the interior with a connoisseur's eye. "Slightly bigger, like I thought. Then again, you are three people and I'm only me."

"I hope you don't mind my asking, but how is the writing going?" asked Melody. Now that she was in the presence of greatness she was feeling more than a little bashful.

"Oh, fine, just fine," he said. He was still turning over his cap in his hands and stood surveying their living quarters with a glint of amusement in his eyes. In fact from where they stood he had a great overview of the entire arrangement: the living space, with a cozy little nook in front of a large fireplace to one side and the kitchen to the other. A staircase that led to a landing and three bedrooms and a bathroom, and of course their pride and joy: a window overlooking the deck, where a large hammock greeted the weary writer.

"Pretty cool," remarked Marty, rocking back on his heels. "How long are you here for?"

"We booked the cabin for the month. We're hoping to finish a rough draft by then. You?"

"I've been here two months now—haven't even finished two chapters. Three more to go."

"Slow going?"

He shrugged. "It's a labor of love. And I love the process. I'm happiest when I'm writing, actually. I dread the day the book is done." He grinned. "Which is probably why it's taking me so long." He spread his arms. "What am I gonna do when it's finished? No idea!"

"You can always write another one."

His smile faltered. "Somehow I have a feeling this is my last one, Melody—can I call you Melody?"

She nodded. "Why would you say that? Of course this won't be your last. You're a writer. Writers write. There will always be a next book—and then a next one after that."

"Sure, sure," he said vaguely, but he was looking a little sad now. When he saw both Zita and Bobbi descend the stairs, both carrying gifts in the forms of a brightly pink e-cig courtesy of Zita and a box of fine cigars courtesy of Bobbi, he almost cried with relief.

"It's my spare vape," said Zita as she handed him the gadget. "I've never used it so it's all yours. It's got the cartridge inside," she added when he opened his mouth to speak.

He held a hand over his heart. "This is more than I could

ever have hoped for. My dear girl. You have saved this wretched writer's life. And you. I love a good cigar."

He tucked the gifts away in the pockets of his cardigan. Then he took Bobbi's hands and pressed them warmly. "How can I ever thank you?" He reached out to Zita and repeated the procedure. "And you. I'll be forever in your debt, Miss Steel and Miss Steel."

"Zita," said Zita.

"Roberta," said Bobbi. "But my friends call me Bobbi."

"Right. Of course." He stood beaming for a moment. "Zita, Bobbi, and Melody. Whenever you want to drop by my place, please do. *Mi* cabin *es su* cabin and all that."

And with these words, he turned on his heel and strode out. And after a final kindly wave—reminding Melody of Santa Claus getting ready to mount his sleigh—he was gone.

Chapter Three

"Sweet man," Melody said as she closed the door.

"Sweet man?" Zita gasped. "Sweet man? He's a legend! Best writer in the world!"

"He's a great writer, sure, but the best in the world? I don't think so."

Zita was aghast. "Of course he's the best writer in the world. He's MSSG! Have you not seen the show?"

"Actually, I haven't," Melody said. "Too violent for my taste."

"*Game of Bones* isn't violent. It's real. It has blood and gore because blood and gore are part of life."

Melody quirked an eyebrow. "Blood and gore aren't part of my life, honey, and I hope to keep it that way."

Zita groaned. It was hard for her to understand how anyone could be this dispassionate about the amazing Marty SS George. His oeuvre was like the bible, an inspiration to her and other writers—in fact he was the reason she wanted to become a writer in the first place. Only in her wildest dreams could she ever have hoped to meet the legendary writer in the flesh, and have him bum a vape off her! She sank down onto the tawny leather couch, her heart beating a mile a minute. This was the greatest day of her life. And she'd played it cool. She'd wanted to hug the man—to kiss that fine bearded face of his—to squeak like a fangirl—but she hadn't. She'd restrained herself with extreme effort.

Bobbi sank onto the couch next to her. "I like blood and gore," she grunted.

"Who doesn't?!" Zita exclaimed. "He's the finest writer on the planet, isn't he?"

"Uh-huh," Bobbi muttered with a frown. And Zita could tell her friend had already forgotten all about the unexpected visit from the literary god, and was back to ruminating about the plot line for Janet Lee Parker's next big mystery.

"Do you think he's out there in that cabin all by himself?"

Bobbi looked up. "Who?"

"Marty. Do you think he has, like, an army of assistants at his beck and call?"

"I doubt it. If he had, he would have asked them to go out and buy him a smoke."

"Makes sense," Zita agreed. "We should visit him soon."

"Uh-huh," Bobbi muttered, frowning again.

Zita patted her co-writer on the shoulder. "Kill off a character. It'll make all the difference."

"But not Snookie."

Zita thought back to Marty's vehemence when confronted with the impending death of the teacup doggie. "Nope. Snookie lives—and he has Marty to thank for it."

EXCERPT FROM MURDER RETREAT (NORA STEEL BOOK 1)

Marty made his way back to his secret lair. Well, maybe not all that secret. Ever since he'd entertained a couple of New York Times reporters last year, the whole world knew where he wrote those massive tomes of his. They'd even snapped shots of the cabin in all of its austere glory. Ever since the article had appeared, every fan in the world had been dying to visit him out here. The upshot was that he'd been forced to move cabins, it being a little tough to write when being harassed by hordes of ecstatic fans every hour on the hour.

He touched the vape in his left cardigan pocket and the small box of cigars in his right pocket and grinned like a kid who's just raided the candy store. His wife Teodora might be a little miffed when she saw him like this, but then she'd never know, would she?

This would be his little secret. Well, his and those three nice ladies next door.

He passed the cabin that used to be his—now occupied by Stan Thurber—and hurried along, hoping Stan wouldn't catch sight of him. He could have asked good old Stan for a smoke, but he was pretty sure he'd rat him out to Teo the first chance he got.

Taking a shortcut through the trees, he hurried along. This was dangerous ground, as *Game of Bones* groupies had been known to camp out here, hoping to catch a glimpse of their idol—or harass him about when the next book in the series would be published.

With surprising agility for a man of his considerable bulk, he cut a clean swath through some rhododendron bushes and came out on the other side, then made a beeline for his own cabin. Once inside, he'd light up and smoke to his heart's content.

And he was so giddy with anticipatory excitement that he didn't even notice the gaunt figure watching his progress through the shrubberies with laser-like focus. The man's skull was angular, his skin almost translucent and his thin lips twisted down in an expression of perpetual disapproval. But it was his eyes that stood out the most: red-rimmed and sunken, they stared at Marty as he disappeared inside his cabin with a searing intensity.

ALSO BY NIC SAINT

The Mysteries of Max
Purrfect Murder
Purrfectly Deadly
Purrfect Revenge
Box Set 1 (Books 1-3)
Purrfect Heat
Purrfect Crime
Purrfect Rivalry
Box Set 2 (Books 4-6)
Purrfect Peril
Purrfect Secret

Nora Steel
Murder Retreat

The Kellys
Murder Motel

Washington & Jefferson
First Shot

Alice Whitehouse
Spooky Times
Spooky Trills
Spooky End
Spooky Spells

Ghosts of London

Between a Ghost and a Spooky Place

Public Ghost Number One

Ghost Save the Queen

Box Set 1 (Books 1-3)

A Tale of Two Harrys

Ghost of Girlband Past

Ghostlier Things

Charleneland

Deadly Ride

Final Ride

Neighborhood Witch Committee

Witchy Start

Witchy Worries

Witchy Wishes

Saffron Diffley

Crime and Retribution

Vice and Verdict

The B-Team

Once Upon a Spy

Tate-à-Tate

Enemy of the Tates

Ghosts vs. Spies

The Ghost Who Came in from the Cold

Witchy Fingers

Witchy Trouble

Witchy Hexations

Witchy Possessions

Witchy Riches

Box Set 1 (Books 1-4)

The Mysteries of Bell & Whitehouse

One Spoonful of Trouble

Two Scoops of Murder

Three Shots of Disaster

Box Set 1 (Books 1-3)

A Twist of Wraith

A Touch of Ghost

A Clash of Spooks

Box Set 2 (Books 4-6)

The Stuffing of Nightmares

A Breath of Dead Air

An Act of Hodd

Box Set 3 (Books 7-9)

Standalone Novels

When in Bruges

The Whiskered Spy

ThrillFix

Homejacking

The Eighth Billionaire

The Wrong Woman

Short Stories
Felonies and Penalties (Saffron Diffley Short 1)
Purrfect Santa (Mysteries of Max Short 1)
Purrfect Christmas Mystery (Mysteries of Max Short 2)
Purrfect Christmas Miracle (Mysteries of Max Short 3)
Purrfectly Flealess (Mysteries of Max Short 4)

ABOUT NIC

Nic Saint is the pen name for writing couple Nick and Nicole Saint. They've penned 70+ novels in the romance, cat sleuth, middle grade, suspense, comedy and cozy mystery genres. Nicole has a background in accounting and Nick in political science and before being struck by the writing bug the Saints worked odd jobs around the world (including massage therapist in Mexico, gardener in Italy, restaurant manager in India, and Berlitz teacher in Belgium).

When they're not writing they enjoy Christmas-themed Hallmark movies (whether it's Christmas or not), all manner of pastry, comic books, a daily dose of yoga (to limber up those limbs), and spoiling their big red tomcat Tommy.

Sign up for the no-spam newsletter and be the first to know when a new book comes out: nicsaint.com/newsletter.

www.nicsaint.com

- facebook.com/nicsaintauthor
- twitter.com/nicsaintauthor
- bookbub.com/authors/nic-saint
- amazon.com/author/nicsaint

Made in the USA
San Bernardino, CA
03 January 2019